THE WRONG SECRET

What you don't know *will* hurt you.

TYLAR PAIGE

Acknowledgments

MiMozas.

Michalle Elizabeth, for all the reasons.

Allie, for showing me strength.

———

Everyone who has supported my crazy goals.

Beta readers Adrianne and Courtney.

Love <3.

Chapter One
A Crime
November 17, 2003

The grass was splashed with fresh blood, and he could almost smell twinges of the sheer fury that had fueled the assault.

He was not supposed to have seen that.

Inside the three-and-a-half-million-dollar home that boasted a lavish interior fit for *MTV Cribs*, two teenaged girls had fallen out. Their argument heated, and the two sloppily slapped each other and pulled at ponytails until one had had enough.

The screaming should have been Myer's first cue to get the hell out of there. But, just as curiosity all too often killed the cat, he found himself staring between the bars of the wrought iron gate that had disrupted his view of... what? He wasn't sure what he'd just seen. His entire body was shaking with disbelief and fear. Fear of losing everything he had worked his ass off for, everything his twenty-six-year-old self had endured to get to this point.

"You knew he was mine! He's always been mine, you bitch! And for God's sake — you disgust me!"

Myer had listened as the brown-haired girl shrieked, her cries piercing a floor-to-ceiling window that fronted a near-colorless room filled with books. They were placed in a disorganized manner on shelves with ladders leaning against them.

"How could I know? I have *never* seen you with him! I … I didn't mean to … d'to …" the other girl stuttered, her thick blonde hair hanging around her petite figure.

"We've been going steady for months!" the brunette yelled. "Don't tell me you haven't seen us together at the mall, the theater, even at Green's! You knew he was mine, stop acting!"

Green's was the local hangout for the high school "in crowd". Every Friday night, swarms of rich kids would drive around the parking lot in their Maseratis and

Porsches, showing off their newly purchased designer clothes and shoes.

A cracking sound split the air — almost like that of a dull blade against asphalt in the middle of a rural neighborhood somewhere in the Deep South. The sound sent a chill down the back of Myer's neck and through to the core of his existence, just below his modestly hairy belly button.

He gasped.

He hurled himself backwards, away from the mailbox behind which he had been hiding his face, so quickly he nearly lost his footing. He was terrified of being caught seeing this gruesome act and having to be involved with it. Still, he couldn't tear his gaze away from the audacity of this girl's actions.

Who the hell could be so malicious at such a young age? he thought.

Myer had only come by to drop off some legal documents for Phil, by way of an overly elegant mailbox — one so spectacular and fancy that it was nicer than Myer's first apartment. Phil's internet music company,

3

which he'd built in the early 2000s, had majorly taken off, and he was now a multi-millionaire living in this Hollywood mansion. It had everything: tall gates, wide landscaping, and concrete fixtures, like lion heads and huge pots with overgrown plants, that likely cost more than Myer's car.

Myer's first major motion screenplay had been picked up by IBC, a picture company in Los Angeles. It was going to be a huge success: Myer felt it deep down in his bones. He was going to *finally* move out of the motel-turned-apartment shithole he'd been living in for three years. The thought of walking out of his front door and seeing anything other than that grimy, green, completely drained pool that likely held fantastic cocaine-and-prostitutes parties back in 1974 was more motivation to get the hell out of this mess.

Phil was investing in Myer's screenplay, *Writing with Knives*; and, in no time, Myer was going to be living the same high life as that douchebag. He just needed his money, nothing else. He certainly wasn't interested in being dragged into court to testify about Phil's daughter and this other girl and whatever had just happened between them.

The blonde, who was at least fifteen pounds smaller than the brunette, scooped up her apparent archnemesis and attempted to throw her over her shoulder. Blood was seeping from the girl's dark hairline; down her pretty, young face; and across her shiny nose ring. As Myer continued to watch, he saw her mouth move.

Blondie quickly dropped her and drew her leg back, aiming for the cut on the taller teen's head.

She began to roll the now-motionless girl through the French doors that led to a foyer. The twenty-or-so-foot runner that once featured in multitudes of galas and parties was going to be drenched in blood, so she kicked it fiercely out of the way. She wrapped her hands and forearms tightly around the brunette's calves, just above her feet, and dragged her across the hardwood floor to the main entry door.

The girl was pulled across the front yard with such care it almost seemed like Blondie had turned into an empath. Before Myer knew it, they'd both vanished from his immediate sight.

He chose to stealthily move to the wooded area just a hundred or so yards down the street. Blondie seemed desperate to figure out what the hell to do, and, try as he might, he couldn't seem to crush his morbid sense of curiosity.

He had barely taken a step before he saw dust particles swirling in the air, thrown into sharp relief by the approaching car lights.

It occurred to him that he had to get the hell out of there and forget he had ever seen that shit go down. The paperwork had already been signed, Myer reminded himself, and no matter what stress Phil might endure over the next few months, the deal was done.

Nothing else mattered.

Chapter Two
A Secret
November 17, 2003

Vinsetta's red-and-gray Nokia phone vibrated in her pocket, and she pulled it out to answer.

"What the hell? Where have you been?" she snapped. "I called you ten times, dude."

"Sorry," Brad muttered. "What's up?"

"I need you to take the car and meet me by the canal at Edgewater, *right now.*"

Brad was nervous, since he didn't have a license; but then again, he already knew how to drive, and Edgewater was only a neighborhood over from his own. He grabbed the keys and ran out the door as fast as he could.

The brand-new, sporty Lexus swept effortlessly round the corners of the winding streets, and Brad soon rolled up to the waterside. Vinsetta waved her hands over her head at him, and he realized he'd better turn the lights off.

He stepped out of the car while it was still running and walked over to Vinsetta.

A look of horror crossed his face.

"Holy shit, what did you do?"

"It was an accident," Vinsetta insisted. "It just happened. Jesus, what do we do?"

The girl's lifeless body lay in the dirt, next to the canal that ran below the mansion. Her dark hair was splayed about her head; her purple overalls were spattered with scarlet drippings, almost like a pattern that some genius designer had made on purpose.

The two of them stared at her.

"This will ruin me. It will ruin us," Vinsetta said under her breath. She turned to Brad. "You have to help me."

Brad had admired Vinsetta since his mom had married her dad a couple years prior. He would do anything for her, and this would, for sure, prove that.

The brunette's hand began to twitch just a little bit, and Brad ran back to the car to grab a blanket from the back seat — the same one that usually accompanied the family on long beachside rides. He grabbed one corner and yanked it, shoveling the rest of it into his arms in a single motion, and carried it back to the bank.

"Here. You do it," he said.

Vinsetta took the blanket from Brad and, without hesitation, pressed it hard over the prone girl's face.

"That should do it."

They stood there, contemplating everything they had just done. They were — or, well, had become — a phenomenal damn *team*.

"Over there." Vinsetta pointed toward the entry gate. "That's where we go next."

"Okay, let's do it."

They walked up the hill, away from the canal, to start taking care of business as planned.

They knew that their actions were nothing short of insane, and they had no idea what to expect: tomorrow, the next days, weeks, months — years, even. But too many lives had been affected by the tragedies wrought by the hands of that pompous asshole. It was clearer than the fancy-as-hell snifter glass that rich asshole drank his whiskey from before he'd force himself upon that young girl he claimed he loved in the wholesome way he should have.

No. To hell with that. Going forward, shit would be better. It would be everything it was supposed to be — and that monster would suffer just as much as everyone he'd hurt, if not more.

X X X

As they arrived back to their brick two-story home in the Lexus, Vinsetta and Brad began to smirk. They carefully walked through the oak front door, their gazes roaming carefully around to make sure that they were, in fact, alone.

The house was silent.

Proud of themselves, as their several-months-long mission was now accomplished. they each exchanged a look, then exclaimed through teenaged giggles, over and over:

"Oh my God. We freaking did it!"

Chapter Three
Aftermath
November 18, 2003

"I'm outside the Eddy family home in Edgewater, where it appears that a serious crime has been committed." The young, attractive news reporter spoke nervously into her microphone as the cameraman started to shoot a live broadcast.

"Mr. and Mrs. Eddy arrived home late last night, after flying home from a private event in Las Vegas, to find their fourteen-year-old daughter, Lauren, missing," she continued. "The presence of a blood trail is leading investigators to believe that this is a case of foul play. The Eddys are offering a five-hundred-thousand-dollar reward to anyone who comes forward with information that leads to the discovery of their daughter."

The cameras were shut off as soon as Mr. Eddy appeared. He stormed down the long driveway, up to the iron gate, and shouted with every ounce of his might at the news crews.

"Get out of here! Get off my property! Leave us alone. Can't you people respect our privacy?!"

The reporter turned to Mr. Eddy, reassuring him that she was only trying to help him and his wife find their daughter, and that her sole intention was to let the public know exactly what had happened. After all, the faster the news spread, the faster they could find Lauren.

If she's still alive, the reporter thought to herself.

X X X

Of course, Myer knew the girl was a goner. He just didn't know where exactly she'd been dragged off to. Maybe the marshes near the fancy-ass neighborhood, down the street? Surely Blondie wasn't old enough to drive — she couldn't possibly have sent them both plunging off a cliff, like a scene from some cheesy-ass, high-school horror flick.

There was no point in even trying to go after a measly $500,000 reward, since Phil had already invested $1.5 million in his screenplay. Plus, the reward was only to lead to her whereabouts, which Myer suspected was not going to end with a hint of the girl's breath.

Myer sat and watched the live report on his 25-inch television, a hand-me-down from a tenant who'd lived there before him. Shivers drilled down his spine as he sucked in a deep breath. He hadn't slept at all since the night before: the night that, one way or another, was going to change his life forever.

He *had* to stay quiet.

X X X

A few weeks later, Myer stared at that same shitty tube TV as the huge, sparkling ball dropped in Times Square and Dick Clark announced the new year. He leaned back in his recliner, sipped his Miller Lite, and told himself that 2004 was going to be the best year ever.

Chapter Four
Formative Years
The 90s

Vinsetta was named after a rich neighborhood, just outside of Detroit, that her mother, Kathy, had always wished she'd lived in. Her middle name was Bette, because that same mother had always adored the famous actress; and, since their last name was Davis, Kathy thought it fit.

Little did Kathy know that her daughter was going to become a silver-screen star herself.

Vin, as most people called her, grew up on the south side of Manhattan. Her dad, Geoff, was a wealthy real estate-monger who had built some of the city's most notable financial institutions in the 1990s and early 2000s. And, when Vin was just eight, he divorced her mother after suffering from repeated abuse at Kathy's hands.

Sometimes, Vinsetta herself was the victim. Other times she was merely in the way, caught in the middle of those typical inter-parent arguments that, in their house, usually turned violent. Her father would have to forcefully restrain Kathy during her bouts of rage and anger, especially when he feared that Vinsetta would be scarred by her mother's psychotic episodes — emotionally, or, more likely, physically.

It wasn't unknown for Geoff to call in help from Kathy's dad, practically begging him to come over and intervene in these fights. Even though she'd been just a kid when it happened, Vinsetta could still vividly recall the urgency in her dad's voice whenever he would pick up the cordless phone to dial Grandpa's number. Kathy would kick and shove him, trying to snatch the phone out of his hands as he frantically stabbed at the buttons.

Grandpa was the only one who had a sure-fire way to soothe Kathy. When she'd submit to her seeming second personality, contracting herself into a corner with her arms wrapped around her knees, she would rock herself while curled up in a ball.

"I don't know who I am. I don't know why I did it. I'm sorry. I'm sorry," she'd snivel as she cried.

As Vinsetta and her father watched what appeared to be the shit horror movies are made of, Grandpa would embrace Kathy with a firm hold. stroking her face and saying even creepier stuff:

"Come back to me, baby girl. Jesus is with you. Come back to me."

Kathy's normally sparkling hazel eyes would, by now, be near black; and Vinsetta would watch in astonishment as they turned back under Grandpa's spell.

This would have been more than enough to screw any kid up in a major way; but Kathy was also a typical narcissist, always trying to find ways to get people's admiration and boost her own sense of self-importance. As a result, she came across as very charming, and was pretty well-liked by those who only saw the face she presented to the outside world. The real Kathy was a far cry from the woman Geoff *thought* he'd married back in 1989, shortly after she had gotten pregnant. They'd married quickly while the stars of being totally smitten were still in their eyes.

Little wonder that no-one could have imagined the insane shit that happened behind closed doors.

Vinsetta was a resilient girl, determined to avoid what she saw as the stereotypical "child victim-turned-adult" lifestyle. She spent her preteen years working with talent agencies that, fortunately, her dad could afford, while also attending middle school. She was even scouted at a young age as a rising star in the film industry, once being told she had a Precious Moments type of dainty face, implying she looked like a porcelain doll.

Her agent, Phyllis, thought so too. She put a more poetic spin on things, though, claiming that Vinsetta had a jawline and cheekbone structure as perfectly symmetrical as a butterfly's wings, and a graceful poise, matched with internal innocence, that caught the eyes of anyone she encountered.

Vinsetta's attitude to all that was a typical tween "whatever". Phyllis was probably just trying to impress Geoff, either to get his money or get in his pants — both of which Vinsetta felt were pretty stupid, since Phyllis always acted so much more immature than her middling age.

Still — perhaps due to her angelic appearance — Vinsetta had already been featured as "the kid" in a couple of made-for-TV movies, nothing A-list. She also rotated through heaps of auditions for teeny-bopper shows like *That's So Jessie* and *Hey, Amanda!*, seeking to get into something with wider appeal.

X X X

Vin's visits with her mother were limited, since Kathy had quickly moved on to her so-called "new supply" — a rugged foreign guy, eight years her junior, who was seemingly naïve as all shit. Considering how potent her lies and manipulations could be, though, it was really little surprise that he'd fallen for them.

That new relationship, perhaps inevitably, turned violent; and Mr. 8-Years-Younger filed charges against Kathy and left. Being exposed for the monster she really was, she felt she had no-one left to believe her bullshit — and she was right.

On February 10th, 2001, just four days before Vinsetta's twelfth birthday, Kathy slit her throat with a freshly sharpened kitchen knife.

Kathy had always had a weird obsession with cutlery. Every few months, she would buy a new set for the kitchen. And she had made several threats to commit suicide in the past — but always empty, always for attention...

It was strange how vividly Vinsetta could recall her walking through the ornate front door, carrying a brand-new box of some overpriced, name-brand knife set. But now, she could hardly remember what her mother's face looked like.

Chapter Five
A Retreat
1999

Geoff reached his arm out to grab the phone from the back of the airplane seat in front of him. Although he was in flight to Los Angeles from New York, he realized he needed to make a quick call back home.

He push-dialed the 212 number he'd had memorized since he was a kid.

"Hi, Mom," he said cheerily when she answered. "It's me."

"Oh, hey, sweetie. Have you landed already?"

"No, not yet. Got about an hour left. But it crossed my mind just now: does Vinsetta have enough of her meds for the week? Can you check?"

"Sure, honey. Hang on. Let me look."

"Thanks, Mom."

There was a clack on the other end of the line as she set the phone down. A few moments later, she returned to let him know that everything was fine with the meds situation, and assured him that she was taking good care of Vinsetta.

Geoff had to be in LA for a real estate investment conference, where he was a keynote speaker; but he also wanted to take a little retreat for himself. It had been over a year since he'd divorced Kathy, and all of it had taken a toll on him to the point where he was desperate for some alone time. As much as Vinsetta was his entire world, he knew she would be in good hands with his mom. After all, she adored her Gramma. They played cards together, and Scrabble; and Gramma would always help with her impending schoolwork, as well as her writing, acting and art.

X X X

Geoff spent a couple days doing all the typical industry bullshit: happy hours and mingling, networking, trying

22

to acquaint himself with potential investors who would be interested in his NYC developments. But after his speech was done, he was ready to get up closer to the north side of the city and relax.

He'd rented a Mercedes Benz convertible for the ride; and, as he drove up the coast, he decided to stop at a little restaurant to grab a bite to eat. Since he'd never eat before a big meeting or speech, he absolutely needed the grub.

It was just about three in the afternoon when he strolled into the cute diner called Geneva's. He probably looked a little out of place in his snappy suit and tie, but Geoff felt right at home. Even though he had a sharp, big-shot exterior, he was the kind of man that was dedicated to his home life, his family — and his work, of course. Sure, he *looked* flashy, but that was nothing more than him trying to keep up with his competitors, so he would look as successful as his clients wanted him to be.

Geoff sat down in the booth, which boasted a classic red, fake-leather back cushion and cream-colored seat, and pulled the laminated menu from the metal holder it was nearly falling out of. The first thing he saw was their *Famous Apple Pie.*

What the hell, he thought. Why not order dessert first? He had no-one he needed to set any sort of example for.

A blonde waitress, who looked like she was in her late twenties, came over and greeted him with a chipper "Hi, there! How are you today?"

Geoff noticed her slightly imperfect smile first, then her sparkling green eyes. She had a warm glow about her, one that you didn't catch unless you were watching the sun rise in a balmy fifty degrees. Something about that shimmer of sun on your face when it is a bit chilly outside just made you feel as if you had found the perfect life balance.

"Uhh, yeah, I'm good," he replied, a little hesitantly. "Thanks. How are you?"

"Same day, different shit," she said lightly. "Know what you'd like to order?"

"Let's start with this apple pie. And a scoop of ice cream to top it off, yeah?"

"That's a hell of a Tuesday afternoon."

Geoff couldn't help but laugh. "What can I say? I'm a dessert first kind of guy. It sucks, because I can't exactly do this in front of my daughter."

"Oh, trust me, I know what you mean. I have a son, and he always wants barbeque potato chips before dinner." She smiled at him again. "I'll get that dessert first for you, and just let me know if you want an actual meal."

"Perfect. Thank you."

X X X

As Geoff delved into the apple pie — which he agreed more than deserved the title of "famous" after a few bites — he took a moment to look around the diner. There weren't many people seated at the tables, and he saw just three people working behind the counter. The girl who had served him was the only waitress.

She didn't seem to be busy enough to make the kind of money it would take to live in a place like this. The neighborhood was pretty fancy, right by the coast; and, although it was a bit off the beaten highway trail, he'd have expected the place to be busier.

Then again, it was three o'clock on a Tuesday afternoon.

Just as Geoff started to carefully spoon the cinnamon-vanilla ice cream from the edges of the bowl, the waitress called out from the counter.

"Ready for one of our famous burgers?"

He whipped around and placed the palm of his hand on the top of the booth. "Famous, huh? Like your apple pie?"

"Yes, sir. All famous on this block, anyway."

He kind of laughed — were there any other restaurants on the block? But, shaking it off, he decided a burger was exactly what his palate needed.

"Bring it on," he said.

"How do you want that cooked? I'm gonna guess medium."

"Damn right. And put all the good shit on it, too."

Fifteen minutes later, she brought out the biggest burger he'd ever seen. It was roughly eight inches in diameter, and smothered with cheese, onions, lettuce, tomatoes, mushrooms, mustard, ketchup and mayo.

"Holy shit!" Geoff exclaimed.

"You said you wanted all the good shit. The only thing missing on that burger now is me."

Her implying that she was "the good shit" made him perk up a bit. Was she flirting with him? Did she say this to all her customers? Or was she just joking around? Geoff had no idea. He hadn't even thought about, or tried, dating in so damn long, he felt pretty clueless.

X X X

Geoff ate the entire damn burger, leaving not even a crumb behind. He yawned just as the waitress slid the bill onto his table, saying, "You can pay this at the counter. See ya there."

Chapter Six
Single Parents
1999

Geoff was so incredibly full he was almost nervous to stand up, fearing that the button on his slacks would bust open.

Is she too young for me? he wondered as he watched the waitress walk back to the counter. *Would she even be interested?*

He had just turned forty-one years old and had his nine-year-old daughter to raise all by himself. But he'd never had a problem attracting the opposite sex. Given that he was such a successful man in the NYC arena of real estate development, and had George-Clooney-type, grizzled good looks, women would swoon over him constantly.

Yet Geoff's priorities had always been his daughter and his marriage — before it ended, of course.

A deep breath and another big yawn later, he went over to her. She was gazing out the window, as if she was daydreaming.

"Hi," Geoff said, with flirty sort of tone.

She smiled at him and said "hi" back.

"Can I ask your name? You've kinda made my day today."

The waitress blushed, her lips pressing together as she tilted her head sideways.

"I'm Elizabeth." She extended her hand across the counter.

"Geoff." He took her hand lightly, only to be surprised by the firmness of her handshake. "Listen: I live in New York, but I'm visiting here for a few more days. I'm not trying to be too forward, but, uh ..." He started to feel extremely nervous. "Could I maybe take you out to dinner?"

Elizabeth was not used to being hit on. Although she had a tight, medium-sized figure, she didn't quite fit the typical LA size-zero mold.

"So ... Really?" She cocked her head so far it nearly touched her shoulder, which had shrugged up to meet her ear.

"Yeah." Geoff smirked, trying to hide his shock that she'd even question someone asking out her gorgeous self.

"Um ... Sure, yeah. When?" Elizabeth asked.

"You mentioned you have a son. I certainly don't want to impose on your time with him. What would be good for you? I'm here until Sunday."

That was five days away.

"That's really sweet of you to consider my son," she said. "He's eight. He's with his dad this week, so I'm free."

Geoff was staying at a swanky, upscale resort about four miles north of Geneva's. He knew there were some great, fancy dining spots up that way, but that didn't seem to be Elizabeth's style. He wanted to get to know who she was and didn't want to go overboard to impress her — or at least not come across that way. He certainly had a lot to offer. His impressive professional portfolio, and his income, could give her that impression if he weren't careful.

"Are you free tonight, or are you working?" Geoff asked.

"I'm off at five, actually."

"Cool. Do you want to meet for dinner around seven-thirty? Maybe somewhere in Butterfly Beach? That's where I'm staying, but I'm happy to come back this way if you have suggestions."

"I know the area. Here, this is my phone number." Elizabeth grabbed a blank check pad near the register, tore off the top page and jotted it down. "Call me after six and let me know where to meet you."

Geoff paid his $23.00 check, added a $10.00 tip, and left with a simple, "Alright. See you soon."

Just before the hydraulic metal door closed behind him, he heard Elizabeth yell out a "see you later!".

X X X

As soon as she arrived home, Elizabeth phoned her friend, desperate to spill everything about this handsome man who'd shown such an interest in her.

"Shit, girl, I haven't been on a date since I broke up with Jarrod … What the…? What do I wear? He seems like a kinda big shot, New York City guy — but he's nice, ya know?"

She decided to just go with it. What did she have to lose?

Twenty minutes into her gal pal pep talk, the call waiting tone beeped. It was either *him* — or Jarrod, which was unlikely, since Jarrod never called her unless he wanted to talk about, or start, some feud over their son.

"Hello?" She'd clicked over.

"Hey, Elizabeth. It's Geoff from the diner."

They made plans to meet up for drinks at a cocktail bar in Butterfly Beach and decided they would go from there.

X X X

Four hours later, they hadn't even left the bar. Their chemistry was insatiable — and, before either of them knew it, they were planning to spend the next few days together.

X X X

Geoff woke up on Friday morning with Elizabeth next to him, feeling on top of the world.

She'd finally spent a night with him in the suite.

He went into the kitchen to make a pot of coffee, grabbed his black flip phone that had been charging beside the coffee machine, and called home to check in.

His mom, and Vinsetta, said that everything was great, and he told them the same in turn — without mentioning Elizabeth, of course. Disappointing, sure; but he knew it was too soon for that.

Almost as soon as he hung up, Elizabeth emerged from the king-size bed and padded into the kitchen, drawn by the scent of freshly brewed, caffeinated goodness floating through the air.

They drank a couple cups of coffee together before she dashed back home to grab her bathing suit for their afternoon beach trip.

"See you in a bit, cutie," she said as she left.

Geoff stayed sitting at the island, staring at the door, as Elizabeth's footsteps receded down the hall.

What the hell is going to happen when I leave? he thought. He'd only known this woman for a few days, but he was totally in awe of her — and he already knew that he didn't want to lose her.

X X X

Sure enough, the two stayed in touch; and Geoff even flew Elizabeth and Brad out to New York for many fun-filled long weekends. When he popped the question about a year later, she, of course, said yes.

Everyone liked Elizabeth right from the start. Vinsetta was nearly ten years old by that time, and Brad was so close to her in age that they clicked really well. After everything she and her dad had gone through with Kathy, Vinsetta felt a sense of belonging with Elizabeth. And, often times, Elizabeth felt more like a fun big sister than a mom figure.

She was, at long last, truly happy.

Chapter Seven
Terror
September 11, 2001

On a sunny Tuesday morning in Manhattan, Vinsetta and Brad had just finished getting ready for school. Vin had just been gifted a beautiful new dress from Elizabeth, which she was excited to parade around the school hallways wearing. Featuring floral colors and black and white stripes and boasting a bubble-style skirt, it was something so fashion-forward she felt like a trendsetter. She paired the frock with some low-heeled black booties that she hoped her size 7.5 feet would never outgrow.

Her shoes clicked against the hardwood floor as they walked towards the elevator door of their penthouse, ready for the three-block stride to middle school.

A sudden crash shivered and jolted throughout Vinsetta's body.

She and Brad looked at each other. The look became a confused stare; and, with one mind, they scurried over to the massive window that overlooked the neighborhood of Tribeca.

"Holy shit!" Brad shouted, his prepubescent voice squeaking.

Their home was on the top floor of the Tower, one of the highest-rise apartment blocks in Tribeca. As such, the plane that slammed into one of the World Trade Center buildings was in plain view.

Vin stumbled across her fancy new boots as she raced to the dining room to grab the phone.

"Where's my mom?" Brad screamed. "Where is she?"

"She's downstairs, she's in her yoga class! Oh my God, my dad, he's at work already. Oh my God, he isn't answering!"

Vin jabbed at the dial pad as she dashed back to the window, fighting to keep her breathing under control.

"Which building is that?" Brad asked, pointing. He and Elizabeth had only moved to New York a year prior, so he wasn't familiar with its layout the way Vin was.

"That's the North Tower, I think. Shit, I don't know ..." She paused; looked out again, trying to get her bearings. "Yeah, it's the North Tower. Dad's in the south!"

Geoff's real estate company was located on the nineteenth floor in the South Tower. Vin continued to dial his number over and over, with no answer, so she tried his cell.

It rang once. Twice.

"Vin!" he answered. "Where are you?"

"I'm home, we're home," she said breathlessly. "We haven't left for school yet."

"Stay there! Stay with Brad and do *not* move!" Geoff's voice shook. She could hear him panting heavily, as well as cries of terror in the background. "I'm on my way out now. What the hell happened?"

Vin broke down and began to cry. He had no clue; and she didn't know what to tell him. She had no idea what the hell had just happened, but she just *knew* she was watching the most horrific accident in the world unfold right before her eyes.

"Vin? Vinsetta, can you hear me?"

"A plane crashed into the tower!" she sobbed. "Dad, Dad, I'm scared. Please come home!"

Silence.

"Dad? Are you there? *Dad!*"

The phone line went dead, and a busy tone rang repeatedly into her newly pierced ear.

Vin slumped onto the bench beneath the window. Brad sat beside her; the two could do nothing but shake, cry, and peel their eyes back and forth from the window to the elevator door.

X X X

After what felt like an eternity, the doors slid open, and Elizabeth darted over to them. She hugged Brad tight, and then reached out to Vin to pull her into her embrace.

The grandfather clock three rooms away began to chime nine o'clock. What was usually a comforting sound to Vin was now competing with the cacophony outside: glass shattering, screams from people in the streets, fire trucks, ambulances, helicopters — thuds of bodies hitting the concrete.

"Elizabeth, those people. Oh my God, all those people …" Vin whimpered as she buried her face in Elizabeth's sweaty tank top.

Brad tore himself away to go turn on the television in the next room. He put the volume up as loud as possible so the three of them could hear the news, even if they weren't close enough to see the screen.

The news anchors were speculating that this was an accidental crash. Every channel was reporting it live. It felt surreal, Vin thought as she and Elizabeth followed Brad. To see this happening in real time on the TV and in her very own front-row seat, right at home.

Vin paced back and forth between the two rooms, looking out at the smoke-filled sky and flames rising from the skyscraper. Just as she approached the window for what felt like the eightieth time, her jaw dropped. She covered her mouth with both of her hands.

"OH MY GOD!" she yelled as chills came over her body. "ANOTHER PLANE!"

Brad and Elizabeth ran in. The second plane was streaking directly towards the towers at what appeared to be ten thousand miles an hour. The three watched as it smashed into the South Tower, the impact shaking every building within a mile radius, including theirs.

"Dad!" Vin shouted at the top of her lungs. "Where is he?"

She curled into a ball on the floor, bawling, screaming for her father. She couldn't breathe. Her body convulsed with anxiety as she gasped for air.

"Where's the phone?!" Elizabeth shrieked, her tone so high-pitched it sounded as if she'd caught the two of them doing something bad.

Vinsetta picked herself up off the freshly steamed oriental rug. Her eyes wandered about the room. She looked over at the table, fixating on the cordless phone that she'd tossed there just minutes ago.

"There!" she said at last.

Brad, meanwhile, was sitting on the couch in a state of shock. He hadn't uttered a word since the second plane had showed up. With his blue eyes fixated on the TV, his face had sunken into a look of absolute disturbance.

Elizabeth dialed Geoff's number over and over; but she, too, continued to get a busy signal.

X X X

The next seven hours felt like fifty years. The three of them sat, huddled together inside what had become a watch house. Buildings collapsed; debris, smoke and soot covered the once crystal-clear glass of every window of their home. The phone line was dead, the power had gone out, and their only hope was that, somehow, this was a nightmare they would eventually wake up from.

Finally, Geoff's soot-and-blood-covered, banged-up, five-foot-eleven frame strode through the door. It was 4:44 PM.

Vin rushed to him as she burst out into tears, surprised she had any left, and felt a near-giddiness that he was, in fact, *alive.*

"I'm okay, sweetie," Geoff soothed. His tone was utterly exhausted. "I, I just — just — I couldn't save them," he stuttered.

Geoff had — as he later recounted I— escaped down the nineteen flights of stairs and spent the entire day roaming the catastrophe-stricken streets, trying to help people and corral them into safe places. Now, though, he just needed to let himself break down, to try and process what had happened.

Elizabeth and Brad rallied around him. Although the four of them had only been a blended family for less than a year, they held each other with nothing less than the greatest appreciation and love. Geoff fell to his knees with anguish, dropping his hands to catch his seemingly lifeless upper body. The sight, and sound, of her ever-strong father being completely defeated by this act of terrorism would haunt Vin for years.

For the next seventy-two hours, this family, along with thousands of others, continued to face further trauma from the tragedy they experienced first-hand, while the rest of the world watched in horror.

Chapter Eight
Starting Over
2003

Early in 2003, Geoff decided it would be best to sell the penthouse and move the family to Los Angeles for a fresh start. Vin was almost thirteen, and the opportunity to work with Hollywood agents to boost her acting career excited the metaphorical shit out of her. She also longed to be part of a more positive community, as New York had become pretty glum since the 9/11 attacks.

She wasn't immediately accepted into the "in crowd" at her new school, as she arrived in the middle of seventh grade. Brad, on the other hand, didn't have any issue making new friends and prospective girlfriends.

She chalked that up to the phenomenon of guys always seeming to fit in quickly. Besides, there were plenty of other kids their age in their modest, modern new neighborhood, living on any given parallel or perpendicular street.

Often, they'd ride their bikes to the next community over, which housed the rich and famous, typically celebrities in fancy-ass, million-dollar homes. It was such a different lifestyle from Manhattan that Vin felt new. Clean. Like *anything* was possible.

Dad and Elizabeth didn't waste any time setting up meetings with potential agents for her. With so much hustle and bustle in the Hollywood scene, there'd never been a better time to bolster her blossoming acting career. They settled on a young, pretty woman named Allie, who was pretty darn genuine and had a no-bullshit attitude.

Vin took to her right away. She was coming into her own, and she wanted a cutthroat "badass bitch" running her career. Not someone like Phyllis, who she'd always felt had her own selfish agenda. Sure, Vin may have only been twelve, but she'd already been through so much bullshit she felt like she was old enough to have a butler serving her wine and cheese.

The girls she went to school with, though, were pretty childish and immature. All they seemed to do was fight over boys; and all they cared about were their appearances, petty shit like who had the prettiest clothes or newest shoes. But Vin already had a career to focus on, so all of it just went in one ear and out the other. Of course, she'd pretend to be interested, at times, just enough to keep a solid reputation in the eyes of the popular girls.

X X X

By the time summer arrived, Vin had landed two upcoming small — but credited — roles in major motion pictures. As her portfolio grew stronger, her highlight reels were starting to get noticed by even bigger producers and casting directors.

Her greatest achievement that year was signing on as the lead in a teen drama-romance movie where a young girl developed a terminal illness, forcing her to question how she would spend the time she had left on Earth. It scored over $3 million at the box office in its opening weekend — and, apparently overnight, she had become a semi-successful, fast-rising actress.

Vin practically made a second career out of keeping her school and professional lives as separate as possible, as most young actors tended to do. She didn't have time to go out with the guys at school, nor did she have the least desire to be like her boy-crazy classmates, embarrassing themselves as they swooned over other, equally pathetic classmen.

There was only one girl that Vin really considered a good friend: someone just as bright and promising, and as totally uninterested in all the drama bullshit as she was.

Chapter Nine
Friendship
2003

Being the new, pretty girl at school meant that virtually all of the other girls instantly snubbed at Vin. But she still managed to strut through the open hallways with a level of youthful confidence that exuded a "don't mess with me" attitude.

Most girls sneered at her, wearing their baby-doll tee shirts and low-waisted jeans; but Lauren, who sat behind her in homeroom, was always kind. She almost had this look of pity whenever they spoke to one another.

Was something wrong with Lauren? Vin certainly felt so. Lauren had this sort of hard-shelled exterior — the kind that was easily cracked open if you had the right tool, like a fake Prada you could buy out of the trunk of a car in NYC. But the presentation was so legit, only someone of Vin's youthful intelligence could see beneath it.

X X X

It was Vin's second week at her new school, and she hadn't even spent the lunch hour in the cafeteria yet. She got used to just going outside with a healthy snack, which she'd pack for herself if Elizabeth hadn't already. She had to keep her appearance cast-worthy, after all.

As usual, Vin was sitting on the little colorful bench, listening to the birds chirping all around her. Turning to toss her wrapper in the trash, she caught sight of the inscription on the bench — it was dedicated to a couple who had been "instrumental in the development of the school's football booster club".

So, some rich old bastards that just donated a shitload of money, she thought.

Just then, Vin became aware of a presence nearby. She whipped back around, her ponytail flying, to see that the girl from homeroom was standing just to the right, and slightly behind, her.

"I'm Lauren," she said quietly. "Mind if I join you?"

"Sure, go ahead. Thanks for helping me with my locker, by the way."

Lauren had given her some advice on her first day that Vin was more than glad to have taken. As Lauren sat down beside her and started to peel a banana she'd pulled from her lunch bag, Lauren started asking her the basics: the typical "who are you?" and "where are you from?" questions.

"I'm from Manhattan," Vin said. "My family and I just moved here a few weeks ago, after 9/11. We needed a new start."

"Oh, I can't imagine what it would have been like to be in the city when it happened," Lauren replied with sympathy. "Were you scared?"

"Yeah. Seeing it from our penthouse, just a few blocks away, was ... pretty shocking. I'm glad we moved here. It was really traumatic."

"You're Vinsetta, right?" Lauren asked, just as Vin realized she hadn't even introduced herself yet.

"Yeah, but just call me Vin."

X X X

From that point on, Lauren and Vin were fast friends. Lauren introduced Vin to some of her own buddies, who were all much more outgoing and personable than Lauren was — at least as far as their outsides showed. They ended up hanging out at Green's together on the weekends and dabbling in some drinking and bong-hitting with eighth and ninth graders.

Weed wasn't really for her, Vin very swiftly learned. She didn't like the way it made her feel: sort of paranoid and powerless. Instead, she'd opt to sip on some cheap-ass wine coolers here and there, or take a little shot of whatever the older kids had their hands on, which never seemed to create a problem. Lauren's choice of booze was always some super-fancy wine she had stolen from her parents' cellar.

They hung out all the time and became damn near inseparable.

X X X

One Friday night in May, Lauren came straight to Vin's place after school for a sleepover. They hadn't made any plans to go to the movies or to Green's that night, but instead were just going to rent a comedy and order in pizza.

As they sat on the front porch waiting for the delivery, Vin finally felt confident enough to ask Lauren about her home life. She'd realized, from the several times she'd visited Lauren's house, that her friend's parents seemed pretty absent from her life. The girls never complained too much about that, since it gave them the freedom to act like heathens, as most middle-school kids will at times. But there was something else — something about Lauren's attitude that had been bugging Vin since the first time she spoke to her.

"Well, I, uh, I have … Uhm," Lauren stuttered. "It's just hard."

"What is?" Vin asked.

"It's just me, you know? I mean, you have Brad. So you aren't alone."

"Uh-huh."

"Everyone knows my dad. He's big-time. Since he's the founder of AutoJam, he's just like, you know, really busy."

"Do you miss him? I mean, what about your mom?"

"Yeah, she's always with him when he travels and shit," Lauren explained. "And then, you know, when she's home, it's like she's just … gone, a lot. Always trying to fit in with the other moms in the neighborhood and at those big mansion parties. It's all new for her, ya know. She didn't grow up with much."

"Oh," Vin said as she sipped on a Diet Coke. She was already becoming accustomed to that sugar-free shit. Pizza wasn't even on her list of "allowed foods" — but then again, neither was a cheap-ass wine cooler or a piss-water beer.

"She likes to … Well, you know … She drinks a lot," Lauren went on. "And … she gets drunk. Then, just, like, doesn't pay attention."

"To you?"

"Yeah, or Dad. Or what he …" She paused. "Just things he does, things I'm not supposed to say."

"You can talk to me, Lauren. I promise I'm your friend for life. Is there something you need to tell me?" Vin coaxed.

"Well … Yeah."

Vin listened as Lauren told her all about how her dad treated her — how he had treated her since she was the ripe old age five. She was in disbelief that a father would do such horrible things to his own goddamn daughter. Then again, Vin's own dad was a freaking saint in her eyes, as well as a hero.

Lauren cried as she skimmed the surface of the disgusting things her father did, the way he would touch her and abuse her. Given her empath nature, Vin cried right alongside Lauren, just as Lauren started to raise her voice a bit.

"I don't want to talk anymore!" Her tone wasn't angry; more an expression that she had shared enough.

"Okay." Vin reached over, grabbing Lauren to give her a hug. "It's okay, Lauren. I'm here for you. I won't tell …"

"No!" Lauren near-shouted. "Please, never tell anyone, Vin. *Ever.*"

They held onto each other for a few minutes, and Vin consoled her friend, raging inside.

She's my soul sister, Vin thought bitterly. *She doesn't deserve this shit, and from her own freaking father…*

Chapter Ten
An Idea
2003

The next morning, Vin woke up next to Lauren; and, before she could even think straight, she muttered the four words that were going to change the rest of their lives.

"I have an idea."

Did she dream it? Where did it come from? Was it because she already felt like she understood Lauren so well that she knew exactly what she needed, even if Lauren herself had no idea? They were just fourteen years old, but they had more maturity than any of the kids they knew at school, even most of those older than them.

Groggy and confused, Lauren opened her eyes and looked at Vinsetta with curiosity.

"Huh?" she asked as she shook to wake herself up.

"You want out?" Vin said quietly. "Like, you really want out?"

Lauren started to whimper a little.

"Yes. I want out."

Vin already had her own money, in her own bank account, from the movies she would star in over the summer. This was going to be easy. All she needed was a well-thought-out plan to get Lauren away from that sicko.

"Drum," Vin said firmly. "He has to know some people."

Drum was a tenth grader who lived on the wrong side of the tracks; but, even so, he was a really cool guy. He was always the one with the drugs at Green's. His real name was Damon, but some drunk guy called him Drummond once, and, as they all laughed it off, the "Drum" part stuck.

X X X

That night, the two of them marched up to Green's. They spotted Drum sitting on the tailgate of his old red Ford Ranger Splash truck; and Vin, without pause, walked directly up to him, on a for-real no bullshit mission.

"Hey, Drum!"

He smiled at her, pushing himself off the tailgate with one foot.

"Hey!" Drum hugged her tight. "How ya doing, girl?"

Vin reckoned the older kids didn't know she was a couple years younger. Regardless, this guy was the type to just befriend everyone: he had a personality made of gold, even if he had some sketchy dealings going on.

"I'm good, dude. Just, uh, I have a favor to ask."

"Yeah, of course. What's up?"

She questioned him on who he might know on that "other side" that might have a small space for rent, was looking for a solid tenant, and would be cool to be paid in cash. Like, legit, not one record in existence of who would be living there —they just wanted the damn money and that's it, that's all.

"Give me a couple weeks," Drum said. "I got you."

Vin skipped back over to Lauren, her jean overalls and pink tee shirt creasing slightly. She patted Lauren's shoulder.

"We're going to do this. And you — you are going to be free."

Lauren sighed. "Okay. And I think, actually, I have an even better idea for making some shit go down. Let's walk."

Lauren told Vin about the most recent incident with her father, and how someone had seen what he did to her that night. Some guy who had missed a meeting with him earlier that day decided to show up at his house to apologize and reschedule. Lauren laid there, staring out the window while her dad stroked himself as he felt her tender, growing breasts — and she saw the man looking directly at her.

She couldn't believe that the guy didn't turn around right then and go to the cops. If he had, she'd have been freed from having to live with her scumbag father in no time.

Instead, the man rang the doorbell.

It deterred her dad from continuing what he was doing to her; so, in the moment, Lauren felt a pang of relief. But after the man left, he came right back into the dining room, where she had just pulled her shirt back over her B-sized bra, and continued where he'd left off.

Lauren had looked out the window one last time to see the guy glance back before he fled down the driveway to his car. She watched as the headlights turned on, the car pulled out, and he was gone.

X X X

The next day, Lauren said, she'd rummaged through her father's office to find out exactly who that guy was. She discovered that her dad was investing in some screenplay, which was a first. She'd never known her dad to invest in any venture that didn't suit him and his selfish lifestyle. What was this was all about?

Either way, Lauren didn't care. She'd memorized the writer's face through the window — and now she'd memorized his name, too.

It sucked that Lauren was unable to turn her father in herself, but Vin understood why. Lauren's fear that she'd have to move into foster care, or worse, seemed to make sense … And if she had to just run away, it would end in her being found for sure. Then she'd have to go back to that house of horrors, and probably suffer even worse abuse at the hands of her dad … Vin knew all too well what that could turn into.

Not on my watch, Lauren. Not on my fucking watch.

"Myer Pone," Vin whispered. "He never did a damn thing, and he's the only person who knows. He needs to pay for what he *didn't* do."

The movie they had watched the night before was called *Uptown Girls*, and they had absolutely loved it. Right then and there, they agreed it would be their code word for talking about everything they'd plotted.

It was going to take a few months to get it all into place; but what was that compared to a future full of freedom?

Chapter Eleven
Favorite Color
2003

Summer came and went in a flash, and Vin made sure Lauren spent as much time at her house as possible. Lauren and Brad had even become closer friends, which made Vin wonder if their bond was more like a teenage crush, a possible romance. She didn't care either way. It just felt like their own little family, a group of people who had each other's best interests at heart, which she knew Lauren sorely needed.

The first month of eighth grade flew by just as fast; and, before they knew it, it was time for the fall fashion show to begin. Their classmates started showing up in boots and long jeans, the days of shorts and flip-flops long behind them. Even though the temperatures never dropped much below sixty or seventy degrees, folks in LA were always fashion-conscious.

Inspired by the movie set Vin had been on for two months, Vin and Lauren brought their own style to school. Wedges and chunky heels were the go-to shoes for their wardrobe, and they'd ditched the traditional fall floral look for color-blocked and striped shirts.

For the time being, they'd tossed aside their heavy plotting; and chose to gallivant like regular teenagers while they still could, with weekend parties, light drinking and flirting with boys to keep their social appearances up being their main priorities. All they had to do was fill time until they found the perfect opportunity to put their plan in place.

X X X

It was Friday, November 14th.

"I heard my dad talking on his cell phone last night," Lauren said nervously. "He's going out of town this weekend, thank God; but I know that Monday night is the one."

Vin asked for as much detail as possible.

"Myer is coming by on Monday night to drop off some paperwork. Dad told him to leave it in the mailbox if he isn't home yet."

Lauren's dad's flight was scheduled to land in the evening, but Los Angeles International Airport was always a crapshoot for staying on schedule.

"What is it, the paperwork?" Vin asked.

"It's a done deal now. Dad signed a couple days ago and delivered it to his lawyer, and now Myer has to sign and return a hard copy to my dad."

"Okay. Your new place is all set. I paid for several years already, so you don't need to worry about rent," she reassured Lauren.

"Oh my God. It's happening. I'm ready."

"You sure?"

"Yeah," Lauren said, although she looked a little like she wanted to throw up. "Is Brad?"

"Let's go over it all this weekend. Just come spend the night with me again."

They walked out of school together and waited for Brad, just as Elizabeth pulled up to the curb.

"Hi, girls. How was school?" Elizabeth asked.

It was small talk the entire way home. Brad sat in the front seat and fiddled around with a bunch of CDs, trying to find one that was suitable for the commute cruise.

Vin looked over at Lauren.

"I don't think I've ever asked, but what's your favorite color?"

"Green," Lauren said. "Why?"

"What shade of green is your favorite?"

Lauren looked perturbed, as if she'd never thought about that before. Vin knew she had a lot on her mind already, so she leaned in and said, with a bit of lenience:

"Just think about it and let me know."

Chapter Twelve
Birthday
February 14, 2022

Vinsetta woke up early, to go for a run, before even checking her iPhone. She figured her social media would already be blowing up with "happy birthday" notifications from fellow actors and industry colleagues on Twitter, and she didn't need to get into that shit just yet. Now, at thirty-three years old, her stardom had reached a point where she was working alongside famous actors whom she'd befriended on various sets.

With a steady pace, she traversed the streets of her modest neighborhood. She nodded a good morning to a neighbor who was out walking with her baby in a stroller, a young man with a smoking-hot body who was also an avid runner, and an older lady with a mangy-looking dog. She noted that she hadn't seen that lady out much, so she must've just moved to the area.

The thoughts racing through her mind were pure and clean and simple: *What am I going to wear tonight? Who's going to show up?* In about twelve hours, she was due to appear at the Lorelei Hotel — specifically, on its rooftop — for an epic birthday party. She'd learned that being single on purpose, husbandless and childless, meant she never had to wait around for someone to make those kind plans for her, or schedule them around shit like babysitters or night shifts.

Needless to say, it'd made for some truly legendary bashes.

X X X

Later in the day, she dropped a bath bomb into her whirlpool tub and waited a few seconds for the water to fizz, watching as it turned a light pinkish color. She stepped into the oversized jet tub and sank her body into the warmth; took a deep breath, followed by a sip of ice-cool Pinot Grigio.

What bath is complete without a glass of wine?

The music she opted for was a bit dark for the occasion — a playlist she typically reserved for long drives to shoots, to gear herself up to be the badass bitch that everyone expected.

Vin was the type to get pretty restless in the bathtub. After only about fifteen minutes of soaking, she began to wash and condition her hair, and cleaned her body as she waited for the conditioner to work its magic. As she ran the loofah over her arms, back and legs, then towards her supple thighs, she felt a bit turned on by the sensation.

Vin let go of the loofah, letting it float around her. She positioned her first and middle fingers between her legs, pressing them against her clit, and started to get aroused.

She felt a pulsation, and a slight twinge of excitement, as she slid her fingers in and out of her pussy, rubbing her clit harder and harder with her free hand. Tilting her head back and closing her eyes, she pictured a tall, dark, handsome man with a beard looking up at her, his tongue teasing every accessible inch of her vulva as he simultaneously fingered the shit out of her. He'd then lick her clit, oh so slowly, and place just the tip of his finger on her asshole, making her come tremendously, visibly, and hard enough for him to taste it.

Vin's entire body shook as she pleasured herself, soaking her fingers with juices only she could enjoy, on this day: her birthday, and also ironically, Valentine's Day.

Feeling so much more relaxed, she stood facing the mirror, dressed in a silk robe, and got all dolled up for the evening. She chose a pink-and-green stunner of a floral dress that she'd purchased at a little boutique called Louisa's. As she slipped it over her head, she reveled in its glory: it fitted her body like a custom-made glove.

One last glance in the mirror as she sipped the last of her wine, and she was ready to call for a ride to head out to the party.

X X X

As Vin walked up the stairs to the rooftop lounge, she immediately noticed a few of her friends had arrived early to start celebrating with happy-hour-discounted drinks.

"Hey, Sage!" She strutted over and gave her best friend a huge hug. "So good to see you!"

The two of them had been best friends for what felt like forever. They were just so alike: no filter, balls-to the-wall honest and forthright — and they *never* missed out on a good time. Sage had recently married a handsome, albeit short, guy named Barry, who she'd met at a New Year's party she attended with Vin a couple years prior. Barry wasn't in the film industry per se, but he was a tax consultant who worked with many well-known stars in Hollywood.

"Happy birthday, girl! Long time no see!" Sage joked — they'd just spent an afternoon together a few days prior.

"Care for your traditional birthday shot of tequila?"

Vin only drank tequila three times a year. One was always at the time she was born, and the clock was ticking closer and closer to this particular moment. The others were reserved for special occasions, like landing a huge new acting gig.

"We've got about twenty minutes, but let's get this shit ready to roll!" Vin said as Barry leaned in with a hug and kiss on the cheek, followed by a "happy birthday".

She turned to the bartender, a pretty brunette girl who instantly recognized Vinsetta and also wished her a happy birthday.

"Three shots of tequila, please."

As she poured three shots and handed them over the bar, Vin imagined that the bartender was a struggling actress — most young bartenders and servers in Hollywood were. The girl's beaming personality shone through in the polite banter she struck up with the group of friends; and Vin was sure it would take her far.

X X X

For the next couple of hours, Vin mingled with friends old and new, laughing and toasting, reminiscing about old times and creating new memories. A guy who'd clearly been drinking all day fell into the planter next to the sofa, while one of the comedians had a group of people laughing so hard that a girl nearly peed herself.

This party was off-the-charts fun, and Vin was so happy to see everyone having a blast.

X X X

Around 9:00 PM, in typical late-as-shit fashion, her agent, Allie, walked through the door. She'd brought a date with her: a man Vin vaguely recognized who was famous for his major motion picture screenplays. They approached Vin arm-in-arm.

"Sorry I'm late," Allie said.

"Are you really, though?" Vin teased.

"Nah!"

They both chuckled as they hugged, and Allie introduced the guy to Vin.

"This is my good friend, Myer."

"Hey, Vinsetta. Nice to meet you." Myer smiled.

"Same here. Great to meet you. Thanks for coming to my party," Vin replied. "Jump on in and grab a drink!"

"Sweetie, why don't you run over to the bar and grab those drinks?" Myer nudged Allie. "I'd love to talk to your friend for a minute. Want anything from the bar, Vinsetta?"

For God's sake — you order Allie around but, in the same breath, try to be polite to me?

"No, thank you. I'm good for now."

Throwing Vinsetta a smile over her shoulder, Allie went over to the bar.

"So, Vinsetta Davis," Myer stated when Allie was out of earshot — rather eloquently, Vin thought, as he fixed her with a discerning look.

Her left eyebrow lifted.

"November 17th ..." Myer mused. "Do you celebrate that day every year?"

Every millisecond shot recalled images into Vin's mind like flashing strobe lights. She was positive she hadn't been able to keep the shock, and disbelief — and fear — from her face.

"I know, Vinsetta." Myer lowered his voice, taking a step closer to her. "I was there. I saw everything. Now, I need you to do something for me. Otherwise, I'll tell the whole fucking world. Plan to hear from me tomorrow. Got it?"

She got it.

Allie returned, drinks in hand, and Myer smiled at her ear-to-ear.

"Thanks, sweetie. Let's party, yeah?"

X X X

The rest of the night was completely thrown off. The knots in Vin's stomach grew tighter and tighter, so much so that she even stopped drinking. She ended up leaving around 10:30 PM — way earlier than she imagined she would on her actual damn birthday.

As soon as she returned home, she texted Sage.

Uptown Girls.

Sage would know exactly what that meant. It was time; and the next couple of months were going to be seriously ugly.

Vinsetta didn't sleep at all that night.

Chapter Thirteen
Matchmaker
February 15, 2022

Vin was not going to let that douchebag ruin her, or anyone's, life. The very next day, after she'd heard from Myer just as he promised, she texted Brad and Sage to fill them in. She needed their help, too— which, of course, she knew he would get.

Her first text was to Brad, but not long after, she copied and pasted the same note to send to Sage.

Watched Uptown Girls this past week. That was our favorite movie, remember?

Oh I remember. He replied. Good times. How was the birthday party?

It was epic, can't wait to tell you all about it! Call me later bro.

It was a signal; one he was sure to understand upon receipt.

X X X

About three hours later, Brad flat-out picked up the phone and called her. Vin told him all about Myer's threat; and, instead of displaying any hint of worry or concern, he just laughed.

"It's gonna be one for the books, right?"

What else could he really say? The plan had been in the works for so damn long; and all they needed now, for this stage, was a mule. That was going to be easy, considering Vin had already done some research that day, and found out that Myer's assistant, Mary, was downright perfect for the job.

Vin had stalked this girl's Facebook and Instagram, learning that not only was she beautiful, but she also had a sort of vulnerable, bright-eyed and bushy-tailed vibe. She totally looked up for a good challenge.

"I've got you booked to play at an event next weekend. You gonna be ready?" Vin asked Brad.

"Heck yeah. Fill me in. Who am I looking for?"

"Okay. She's a bit on the taller side from what I can tell. Maybe five-foot-six or five-foot-eight. She's biracial; got a gorgeous skin tone. Long, dark hair. She's pretty stylish, so I expect she'll be dressed fashionably. I'd send a pic, but, you know, probably not a good idea."

"Yeah, I got you," Brad reassured Vin. "Anything else?"

"Well, it looks like her last relationship ended about eight or nine months ago. Hard to tell, but she hasn't posted a photo with a guy since then, and someone commented that they were a cute couple. So, yeah, it wasn't her brother or anything."

"Cool. Where and what time?"

Vin recited the details directly from the event's Facebook page, where she'd seen that Mary had RSVPed "yes" to the concert. It was at a smaller venue in Brentwood Park, and Mary had even commented and posted on the page and tagged a couple friends. She must know one of the acts who were headlining, or something like that.

But Vin had serious clout — and that meant she could get away with shit most other people couldn't. She called the owner of the place and asked if her "very good friend" could open with a short set. If he could, she would show up herself and bring several of her big-shot actor friends.

He didn't hesitate to agree, since all it meant for him was adding an extra fifteen or twenty minutes to the opening of the show. No big deal. And, in terms of online exposure, having an actress with over 500k followers on Instagram posting from his venue's show would be priceless.

X X X

The night of the show, Brad and Vin met up outside. Not that he needed a pep talk at all — they'd been preparing for this shitshow since they were fourteen. Either way, she wasn't going to let him do this all on his own. She would be there for him, like he'd always been for her, like they'd always been for each other.

Just as promised, Vin brought a few friends: Sage, of course, and a couple other girlfriends who were also in showbusiness. They even got a bit of special treatment, being offered seats right up front.

"Here we go," Vin said to Brad as he approached the backstage area. "I think I saw her already. She's at the bar with two friends."

"Where?"

Vin nonchalantly pointed in the direction of where Mary was sitting.

"Ah." Brad's eyes widened a little. "Holy – damn, you're right. She is gorgeous."

"Atta boy. Get her."

X X X

Brad took to the stage just thirty minutes later. As he sang one of his best songs, *The Winding Road,* he dedicated it to the beautiful woman sitting at the bar.

Vin looked back, just like everyone else, to see who he meant. Was it someone he knew? Was it a stranger?

X X X

Mary and her friends were looking around, trying to work it out — and she even thought, just for one second: *Could it be me?*

Nah.

Mary had never regarded herself as particularly beautiful. And, having grown up in a smaller town further north, she'd felt pretty ignored for most of her life.

Still, it was nice to imagine.

As the guy on stage — Brad — strummed the last chord on his guitar, he said, "I don't know your name, beautiful girl in the purple shirt, but I soon will."
Holy shit.

X X X

Once Brad left the stage, though, he needed to play it cool for a few before heading out to the audience area. What good would it do if he immediately went out to seduce her? That would be way too over-the-top.

So, he had to make Mary wait, had to build some anticipation — with her, and with her giddy-ass friends, who were surely all giggly and flustered over their girl being moments away from meeting this up-and-coming country-rock star.

He handed off the guitar to one of the sound guys. Downed the last of the bottle of water he'd been given to take on stage. Checked his phone.

It was time for him to get this shit going.

Brad made his way over to the bar; and, as he did, he saw Mary looking directly into his eyes. Not at his body — right in his overwhelming eyes. He felt a pang in his dick, as if she was already riding it.

"Hey, I'm Brad," he said smoothly, leaning on the bar and reaching out his hand.

"Mary," she said, gazing up at him. He might have just been imagining it, but Brad could have sworn her face lit up when they shook hands.

Mary's two friends introduced themselves one at a time. He nodded to each of them, as if to tell them they were also beautiful, but not *quite* as beautiful as the girl he had his eye on.

Is she really this stunning? Brad thought. *Or am I just making shit up because of what Vin told me?*

"What brings you here tonight?" he asked her.

"My friend Sue's brother is headlining," Mary said, a tinge of excitement in her voice, "so we're here to support him."

"Well, I saw you while I was on stage, and I couldn't take my eyes off you."

Mary blushed and put her head into her hands, shaking it side to side as she half-laughed. "Really?"

"Hell yes! I don't know who you are, but I want to."

Mary's friends excused themselves to go move a little closer to the show, since they had VIP seats and had only been sitting at the bar to grab drinks.

"Girl, please — keep your ass right here!" Sue said, with a nod and wink of approval.

X X X

Mary felt like a bit of an asshole for letting her friends go up there without her, but they insisted they'd save her a seat. She wouldn't be long, right? Just a little flirty banter with this hot, guitar-playing guy …

Two hours of engaging conversation later, Mary still hadn't had enough. She was totally enthralled by him; and, judging by his reaction, Brad wanted more, too.

Chapter Fourteen
Discovery
March 15, 2022

It was a perfect, clear-skied, seventy-degree evening in Beverly Hills. Brad had been working behind the bar for three hours already and was feeling a little restless. Swarms of gentlemen would usually pile in for cigars and bourbon during these weekly Happy Hours, but this particular night was much slower.

He was bummed his tips wouldn't be as much as usual, since they were all he had to support himself financially, renting a studio apartment while he struggled to get his musical talent noticed. Granted, he was a rock-country guitarist and singer-songwriter, so most people would expect him to live in a city like Nashville. But he'd been brought up in the LA scene. He felt he knew it pretty well and was comfortable trying to make it there.

At eight o'clock, two middle-aged men walked in.

"Two San Cristobal Elegancia and two Blantons, please," the taller of them requested.

"Sure thing." Brad stepped out to the humidor to fetch the smokes, then came back to the bar to pour two glasses of bourbon. He slid the drinks over to the men, along with a cutter and the two cigars.

"Anything else?" he asked as the two customers were chatting.

"Yeah. What's the deal with you?" said the shorter, stockier one.

Brad chuckled, looking at the man with interest. "What do you mean?"

"You're a good-looking guy — what, about twenty-five? Why are you working here? Catching a vibe you're looking for more, I suppose."

Brad had been working at the lounge for a couple years now, and this was the first time he'd seen these two come in. It was typically pretty packed with regulars.

He was, needless to say, intrigued.

"Well, I'm a musician," he replied. "Have been for ten years. But I'm not twenty-five. I'm thirty-two. I just haven't found my path yet."

"Ah, I see. What kind of music do you play?"

"Mostly country. Sorta rock-country."

"And you think you're gonna make it big, as soon as the right opportunity comes along, right?" the tall man chipped in.

"Fuck yeah, I'm going to make it." Brad's tone was confident. "This shit takes time, and I'm patient. I know I have to be to make it."

They all laughed. The tall guy reached into his back pocket, pulled out his expensive-ass wallet, and poked at the inside flaps with his fingers.

"Eh, I don't have a card on me. But here — take my number, my man," he insisted. "I'm a talent agent. I don't work with country musicians, but I'm digging your energy. Let's set up a meeting."

"Uh, damn, dude, for real?" Brad was in shock. "Hell yeah."

He took out his phone, punched in the number the man recited, and sent a text that just had his name.

The two men moved away to situate themselves on a nearby sofa. As they did, the tall guy looked back at Brad and said, "Talk soon, my friend."

Brad realized, too late, that he hadn't caught the guy's name; but he still felt a sense of success and couldn't wait to text Vinsetta.

OMG. This big-shot agent just asked me for a meeting!

What??!! How did that happen? So cool! she replied.

I'm working the bar, and these two high rollers walked in and started chatting with me. Next thing I knew, he was asking to hear my shit!

So proud, bro. So awesome!

X X X

The next day, Brad woke up earlier than usual. His nervous energy matched his excitement as he wondered if it was too soon to text the dude.

Probably. But he could at least spend some time brushing up on his latest songs, so he was ready to rock that guy's world when they met.

Brad spent some time fiddling through his songs, picking out the ones he felt most confident about.

"Wesley, Don't Tempt Me."

That was one of his favorites. It was about a girl who was secretly in love with her boyfriend's brother. Kinda messed up and twisted, but it hinted at the old philosophy that "True love can't be found where it doesn't truly exist, nor can it be hidden where it truly does." That was an old François de La Rochefoucauld quote; one that had stuck with him since he was a kid, when he'd heard it on some rom-com movie he probably shouldn't have been watching at that age.

Yeah. That was the one.

X X X

Later that day, Brad picked up his cell phone and went to his recent call log. The dude's number was right under Vin's. His hands shook a bit as he started to click through to call the number.

Wait, he thought. *Should I text?*

Nah. Calling was way bolder a move — more ballsy than just sitting behind some letters.

His finger hit the call icon, and he cleared his throat quickly. It was 3:31 PM on Wednesday.

The phone rang exactly three times.

"Mr. Case," came the deep voice on the other end.

"Hey, Mr. Case," Brad said, relieved that the guy had answered with his name. This is Brad, I was, uh, your bartender last night at Circle Cigar Lounge."

There was silence for a couple seconds.

"Oh, yeah!" Mr. Case exclaimed. "How ya doing, my friend?"

"Ha, I'm good. How are you?"

"Another day, another damn dollar, right?"

"Yeah, I hear ya. I was calling to see if we could set up that meeting. I've got some really cool shit I would love for you to hear."

"For sure, man. What's your day look like tomorrow? I just had some asshat cancel on me at 10:00 AM. That work for you?" he asked.

Brad had stars in his eyes so damn bright he would have yes to meeting in an alley in a shady neighborhood at 3:00 AM.

"Yeah, for sure! Where am I headed?"

He jotted down the address, hung up the phone and started jumping up and down. He soon took to Google to research Mr. Case, and quickly learned just *how* big this bigshot really was. In short, he was *the* bigshot he needed for his music to finally be noticed.

Even though this was nothing promised, it was definitely a start to something — Brad could feel it deep down.

Chapter Fifteen
The Arrival
April 6, 2022

It was a snowy Wednesday morning in Manhattan, and the temperature was a bit unseasonably chilly, just cold enough for the rain to freeze into oversized, individual flakes.

Vinsetta's flight had just arrived at John F. Kennedy Airport. As she exited through the sliding glass doors, she felt the familiar chill against her face, wrapped a scarf around her neck, and took a deep breath.

She was about to embark upon the biggest acting job of her career.

With cash in hand, Vin hailed a taxi, deciding not to take an Uber. The driver, a man with an Indian accent, made small talk, and she bantered back politely in one- or two-sentence replies.

Although she was a well-known, B-list Hollywood actress, the guy didn't recognize Vin, which was of instant comfort to her. She felt her stomach tie itself into a knot as they drove through the upscale neighborhoods she once gallivanted in as a young girl.

X X X

They arrived at the flat that had been arranged as her rental for the next week, which was situated in the center of the West Village. As Vin hoisted herself from the right-side door onto the city sidewalk, she grinned. She pulled her magenta overnight bag and light pink carry-on from the back seat, handed the driver the $67.00 fare, and turned to look up at the building where she knew she was going to make someone — no, everyone — exceptionally happy.

Vin walked, with her unusually light luggage in tow, up to the stairs, where she was all set to meet the Airbnb host. As she waited, she grabbed her phone and checked in with Mary.

Hey, just arrived, she typed. Waiting for Lark to show up.

Ok, great. Let me know if there are any issues.

Will do.

Vin stood and waited for nearly fifteen minutes while the snow encircled her. It felt like the entire world passed her by as people scurried through the streets around her.

She was scrolling through the most recent comments she'd received on Instagram when she felt a presence nearby and looked up from her phone. A strikingly handsome, rugged man walked around the corner a mere fifty or so feet from her. He didn't have the cliché appearance of a New York City resident: he wasn't slick or sleek with his hair or his wardrobe.

His six-foot-two frame approached the stoop with a seemingly less-than-confident attitude. His light brown hair, sprinkled with salt-and-pepper strands, was tousled, much like that of a stereotypical hockey player. He had deep, brown eyes that, although they looked nearly yellow in this light, didn't unsettle her. He looked at her with a gaze that was reminiscent of a soldier returning home from war to set eyes on his beautiful wife for the first time in a year.

Vin quickly recognized him: Larkland Rozsak. The guy was a well-known, *NYC-Times*-best-selling author, whose works were published at-large by a major local book company. He penned mostly thriller and mystery fiction novels and was known to live "under the radar" so much that his fans, and peers, never knew who he really was. He managed to keep his private life exactly that — private.

As such, Vin didn't let on that she'd figured out his identity. Not even a little bit.

Larkland stopped directly in front of her, almost towering over her five-foot-five, 130-pound frame.

"Hey, I'm Lark," he said — ever so humbly, yet with a slight touch of arrogance. "You ready to see the place? It's pretty badass."

He knew who Vin was. She was sure of it.

She gazed up at Larkland, flashing him a quirky smile. "You bet. I'm Vinsetta, by the way. And I'm kinda 'badass' myself."

Even if he does know, she reminded herself, *I can't let it get to me.*

They went up the seven steps together, side-by-side, which Vin found to be a bit odd. Typically, she'd follow closely behind the other person. Larkland hadn't offered to take her bags, either. Maybe he was trying to make it clear that he wasn't interested in being a gentleman, for fear he'd come across as expressing a more-than-cordial interest in her.

After walking through the main corridor and up two flights of stairs, they walked into the 900-square-foot apartment, which Larkland had called his "author loft" in his correspondence with Mary.

The place was unbelievable. It had 20-foot ceilings with exposed brick and ducts, and floors splashed with drips of paint — no doubt from their being left carelessly uncovered during redecorating. It was a beautiful disaster, almost. The windows were uncovered, too —

odd for an apartment on the second floor. Nearly anyone walking by could see clear into the space: the one large, open room divided into a bedroom, kitchen and living room, all of which were within just a few feet of each other.

It was perfect for an author. Cozy black-and-white chairs and writing nooks were nestled up in several places, set out as if moving just a few feet would take him to an entirely new country. Vin also noticed journals everywhere and writing pads with pens shoved inside them scattered about in random spots.

A true writer's life, she supposed. Were all authors this messy? It was clean, no doubt; but she could immediately tell this was where Larkland would get lost in his own words and stories.

Intrigued by her – no, *his* – surroundings, Vin was more than ready to be part of his next story — one that was likely going to be majorly fucked up from this day forward.

Chapter Sixteen
The Loft
April 6, 2022

Vin set her bags down just to the left of the bed, on an old trunk that looked like it was from the 1920s. She really appreciated the blend of antique furnishings with that stereotypical "manly man" monochrome style. Larkland was standing in the kitchen, rattling off some instructions for taking care of the place while she'd be there; and so, Vin pretended to listen while taking in the view from the window.

"I love this street. It's quiet for Manhattan," she said, watching the snowfall come to an end.

"It is nice here. And it's peaceful for what you'll need for the week," Larkland confirmed. "I think you'll love it. Feel free to make yourself at home — sleep in the bed, or on the pull-out sofa if you like. Both have new bedding ready for you, right here." He lifted the lid of a small ottoman, revealing crisp white sheets and pillows.

"It's not very colorful here, I know," he continued.

"That's okay. I have too much color in my life most days," Vin chuckled. "This is a perfect change. I just needed to get away and feel at home again."

"As we all need to do sometimes. This is my home — where I live is just where I live. Kinda funny how there's a difference, you know?"

"Oh, I do know. I feel like all I do is travel for work,and stay in hotels. Although I live in Los Angeles, it'll never be home like New York." Vin let out a sigh, before pulling herself together. "This is a cool fucking place, I really dig it. I'm sick to death of hotels and fancy shit."

"Well, if you need some really un-fancy shit, let me know," Larkland said. "My friend owns a fun little dive bar not far from here. It's a host of mixed nuts and not a single beer over five bucks."

"Um, hell yes. That is exactly where I want to be and exactly what I need to do. I can't wait to ditch my Dolce and Gabbana heels, put on my Amazon Essentials flip flops, turn my phone off and go sing some karaoke."

Larkland laughed audibly. "Karaoke? Who said anything about karaoke?"

"Uh, me! I want to sing karaoke. Hey, I might be a great actress and dancer, but I can't sing for shit. That's why I will never be a triple threat!" Vin shook her hips and snapped her fingers to show him a quick preview of her best dance moves. "And let's face it: karaoke is the best place to let loose and suck at what I suck at. It's all okay, because most other people suck at it, too."

Larkland laughed again as Vin joined in with a few chuckles too.

X X X

They exchanged cell numbers just before Larkland left her alone for the afternoon. As Vin typed his name into her phone, she felt his shoulder lean just close enough for her to catch a whiff of his scent.

"Call me Lark," he insisted.

Vin had already typed out his full name, so she backspaced a few letters. Even though this, surely, was not a nickname or a pet name, a part of her felt a first victory. It was his personal preference. *Personal.*

She needed to return a similar touch, so she grabbed his phone and keyed in her own name as *Vin Bette Davis.*

The snow had just completely stopped, and Vin watched out the window as Larkland strutted his fine ass down the street. She imagined he was off to his big, success-ridden, lavish apartment that was walking distance from this beginner-writer-turned-author's loft.

Vin wondered what it looked like, and if he would invite her to it. Did it have a feminine touch at all? Had he ever been married? Did he hire an interior designer? She couldn't wait to get inside his head, since that was the whole point of her mission — and there was no denying that she equally couldn't wait to get inside his pants.

Chapter Seventeen
Zelda
April 6, 2022

Vin wanted to curl herself up into a ball with one of the unusually soft blankets she'd discovered, in a pile, on a papasan chair next to the TV.

Instead, she began to snoop.

Vin found herself flipping through every journal, notebook and notepad she could find, looking for clues about this mysterious author who now had her full attention. She managed to find a few anecdotes: nothing particularly interesting, though.

He'd had a dog named Zelda, a bulldog boxer rescue who became too old to live comfortably and who he'd had to put down. Sad, for sure — but not what Vin was looking for. She did enjoy the way he'd written about his furry friend, though: as if Zelda was actually a part of his own identity.

My Zelda. My reflection, my mirror, my animal. You were me, and I was you. When I hurt, you hurt. When you hurt, I hurt. The pain you felt was the pain I felt. The moment you had to go was the moment I had to go.

I held your paw in mine; caressed your ears, as you always loved; looked deep into your soulful, beady eyes as you took your last breath and closed them for the last time. As you lay before me, I suffered your suffering and celebrated your freedom.

I went with you to Heaven, just for a moment, to make sure you were okay. You turned, to wiggle your butt and nudge your head in between my knees, before you pranced off into the white distance. And I knew your rainbow had carried you to the pot of gold that neither I, nor this world, could ever give you. The one that would be eternal, painless and free from the shitty-ass humans that would never look at you the way you deserved to be looked at — with compassion and excitement.

I will always be your human; you will always be my animal. Enjoy your endless prancing on rainbow-colored streets, and all the peanut-butter treats.

Vin wanted to cry a little bit — that was such an awesome sentiment. But she had to stay the course here. No time for tears.

Drawers. There were lots of drawers. She carefully dug through each one, in the kitchen, the bathroom, the armoire that held the massive 70-inch HDTV. She found that most had standard guy things in them: a tiny sewing kit; some old cologne bottles; koozies that had been weathered from obvious boat outings; knick-knacks like bottle openers, Advil, a groomsman flask, cheap-ass coasters — and an extra-large-sized condom that expired in 2017.

Where could she find something that would tell her more? She was all alone in a $1,100 a night Airbnb, so she didn't fear getting caught.

I'm free to be as crazy a bitch as I want, Vin thought. *And, holy crap, am I going to be.*

Suddenly, her phone vibrated against the kitchen counter where it was charging. She stopped rummaging through random shit to go check it, hoping it was from Lark.

It was from Mary.

Everything go good with check-in? All set? Any problems?

She'd already told Mary that she would let her know if she had any issues. Vin assumed Mary just didn't really know her well enough to understand her Type A personality, so, she replied:

I'm here, all good. Think I successfully made plans to hang out. Will keep you and Myer posted.

Her phone buzzed again a moment later.

Fantastic, I'm leaving town tomorrow with my boyfriend so pls keep Myer in the loop.

Mary had mentioned, when they'd met up a few days prior, that she was taking her new guy on a big trip. Obviously, Vin already knew he'd landed that record deal, but she couldn't let on. So, she let Mary gush all the details about it and reacted with a matched-up level of excitement. As a spunky twenty-seven-year-old new to the LA scene, she wasn't surprised that Mary and Brad had hit it off so well.

X X X

Next, Vin decided to peek into the kitchen pantry and, ultimately, the fridge. She was itching for a glass of wine, but anything would do at this point. She just wanted to relax and take the edge off the day. Shit, even some hard liquor would do the trick, although she rarely ever drank that.

She found an old-ass bottle of Four Roses bourbon and figured that would have to do. Interesting — was that Larkland's drink of his choice? Or had someone else been there and left it behind? The label was clearly mangy and scuffed; and, if Vin's first impressions had been right, he hadn't really spent much time in the loft in a while.

Either way, bourbon it was.

Vin opened up three or four of the cabinets before finally finding bar glasses, which were, surprisingly, very elegant. They even had his initials etched into each one: *LJR*. She poured herself a full glass of the shitty old whisky and started to drink.

What could J stand for? Vin's mind wandered, curious. Josh, Joshua? Nah, that was too common for a name like *Larkland*. But, wait — what if Larkland wasn't his real name? What if it was something like Larry or Lowell?

Lowell? Oh, fuck, the bourbon is getting to me already.

Of its own accord, Vin's mind began to create a "to-find-out" list about Lark. Middle name was definitely one of those things. After all, that was the sort of intimate detail someone usually only shared after they'd *really* gotten to know someone …

Chapter Eighteen
Drunken Pig
April 6, 2022

Vin sat on one of Larkland's plush chairs, in a bit of a daze after two glasses of bourbon. Her phone lit up, and she glanced over to see Lark's name on the screen.

Pretty zealous. He only left a couple hours ago.

Maybe he was just as anxious to explore their possible chemistry as she was. Or was he just bored? Either way, Vinsetta didn't give a shit.

Hey, how is the place treating you so far? he'd asked.

It's great, thanks. I busted out the bourbon, hope that's okay.

Haha, of course. Tired? Or feel up to having another drink with me at The Drunken Pig?

Well, shit, she thought. *Here we go.*

Vin wasn't typically one for much rest — her life had always been go, go, go. And even though she had a lot of plotting and planning to follow, she also knew she needed to let go a bit, let things happen. One thing she'd learned as an actress was that getting into character meant relieving yourself of your natural tendencies, in order to make your role believable.

Drunken Pig it is. How's 8:00?

Larkland's reply took several minutes to arrive, during which Vin pondered a bit. It seemed as if he'd just abandoned their dialogue right in the middle of making plans. Eventually, though, he did confirm what she'd suggested. He also let her know that there was no karaoke that evening, which she thought was cute. If things went well, perhaps they would save that for another evening of impromptu shenanigans.

X X X

Vin had already unpacked her light suitcase, and carefully unfolded her clothes to pile on top of the dresser next to the bed. She'd also packed a couple of dresses in anticipation that she might need to look extra cute. Was this that time? Or would the name "Drunken Pig" alone imply that jeans, boots and a sweater would suffice? She didn't want to look like she was trying too hard — rather, just keeping it casual, as if she were meeting a friend.

Vin sat on the bed and pulled on her dark-blue jeans that had a couple of intentional rips in them. She paired them with a white, long-sleeved top and tan boots, and covered that with a green-and-white floral designer peacoat and pink scarf. Even though it was April, it was cold outside, as the sun had already set.

She stepped out into the hallway, closed the door and locked it behind her, and trekked down the stairs to exit to the street.

X X X

The map-app directions showed she was just eight minutes away from The Drunken Pig. So, in true actress-going-wild fashion, Vin dug into her cross-body bag and pulled out a cigarette to smoke while she walked. Of course, it wasn't something she'd indulge in often; but in this scenario, she was in total carefree mode.

She noticed the lights on every block of the city were glaring — seemingly at her, as if to say "where the hell have you been, Vin?". As she walked through the semi-quiet neighborhood, down to a bustling street filled with tourists, she double-checked her phone to make sure the little blue dot — her only companion in that moment — was going the right way.

She was only steps away from destiny.

X X X

The dim, buzzing, pastel neon sign that read *The Drunken Pig* looked like it was hanging by an unraveling piece of twine. The door it hung above was barely even red anymore.

Vin could tell this place had surely seen good times; and its clientele clearly wasn't made up of much more than some tourists on the hunt for a dive bar, where they'd find locals, possibly some pool sharks, and sports on TV. She stepped up and over the stoop, where she imagined at least a few people had tripped in drunken states, and entered the bar.

It was 8:02 PM.

Larkland was already perched up on a stool at the bar, looking stupid devastatingly handsome. The first thing she noticed was that he hadn't changed his clothes from earlier. How in the world did Myer know that she'd have such crazy chemistry with this guy? Or was this just his way of torturing her, since the outcome wasn't going to be good for either herself — or Larkland — unless she did exactly what she was supposed to do.

Ugh, fuck my life. Whether it was just lust, or whether it turned out to be something more, she had to put it aside.

X X X

Two hours, four drinks, and loads of conversation later, they found themselves pretty tipsy and feeling like they wanted more fun.

"What's nearby?" Vin asked over the noise. "Other than more bars, of course."

"My place," Larkland yelled back. "I just live a couple blocks from here. Want to come over, or is that against your first date rules?"

Ahhh, crap.

Vin felt a little relieved — he was definitely interested, which meant she was going to be able to get to the nitty-gritty, dirty shit faster. And, despite everything, she'd have loved to consider this one of those situations where the connection was just so damn strong, no words needed to be spoken about the fact that it was a date.

Still, she'd have to question it if she wanted to come across as mysterious and well-behaved, like she intended.

"Date?" Vin raised an eyebrow. "I didn't realize this was a date."

"Well, isn't it? I mean, don't mess around with me, Vin. We had an instant spark earlier, didn't we?"

She laughed and gave him a nod of approval, certain that she had a massive glowing sparkle in her eye.

"I suppose so."

"In that case, I have a pretty vast selection of just about anything your liver could desire back at home."

"Uhhmm …" Vin contemplated as she looked down at the rose-gold Michele watch she'd chosen to complement her fairly plain outfit. "It's only a few minutes after ten, so yeah. Screw it, let's go."

She'd had enough of the bar scene at this point, anyway, and was ready to go somewhere they could relax a bit. But she wondered if she was drunk enough to really relax, or if she was putting herself in danger of revealing, even in the slightest, that she had some ulterior motive.

She threw caution to the wind and followed her instincts, which were being led largely by hormones and partly by her mission. She needed to gain his trust, but also didn't want to lose his respect.

Larkland said goodbye to his buddy, who was working the bar; then he and Vin exited back out the front door. Taking care not to trip over the stoop, they went off to his apartment.

Chapter Nineteen
Seduction
April 6, 2022

All of a sudden, Larkland was a gentleman. He pulled Vin's coat off her shoulders as she shimmied out of it, and she turned around to see his beaming face.

"A drink?"

Vin nodded, and he smirked.

They walked through the foyer and past Larkland's fancy living room to the dining room, which was less "dining" and more "drinking". He'd clearly not been interested in hosting much, as the traditional dining room was set up as a bar.

Vin took a seat atop a stool that had rich blue velour upholstery.

"You said you had a big selection," she said. "How about a scotch — neat?"

"You got it."

As Larkland poured the drink into a bland rocks glass he'd pulled from the cabinet, Vin told him about her last acting gig and the insanity that went down on set. One of the actors that she had worked with was in the middle of a crazy custody battle with his ex-wife, and he made sure everyone knew every detail as-it-happened. It just made her even happier that she'd never married or had children.

Eventually, Larkland cracked himself open a local brewery beer and sat down on the neighboring stool.

"How does it feel to be back here — home?" he asked, his eyes gazing right into hers.

Vin hadn't told him that New York was ever home for her, so her back arched a bit as she tilted her head slightly.

"I looked at your IMDB profile," Larkland laughed.

It confirmed what she'd known, really, right from the start. And weirdly enough, she didn't care.

"Ah, yeah," Vin said, "so you know I was born and raised around here. Glad to hear you took an interest!"

"Well, I knew who you were as soon as I saw you. I didn't want to creep you out, but I've watched some of your mediocre movies!"

He laughed, legitimately and out loud, and Vin laughed in concert with him.

Then came a moment of silence — the kind where Vin couldn't be sure if her heart was even still beating or if she'd gone deaf. It was like one of those crazy, surreal moments where she'd looked at a clock with a second timer and it felt as if that second number was lingering for minutes.

Lark's lean into her was nothing short of breathtaking, and Vin almost felt him thrusting against her body just from the look in his eyes. There was a momentary pause as his forehead met to hers, where they looked at each other with an almost dead giveaway of motive …

Nah, he doesn't know, Vin thought, taking hold of Lark's jaw and bringing his mouth to hers.

Vin had already resolved that, even though she had this truly insane chemistry with Lark, she wouldn't let it go too far. But that indulgent first kiss felt like the conviction of a thirty-something-year-old unsolved mystery.

They soon found themselves passionately making out against the dark-blue wall of Lark's bar room. Vin felt his hands start to gently caress her thighs — right before he grabbed her ass in a swift, firm hold. It was the perfect mix of subtle and aggressive, and her knees began to go weak as she ran her hands under his tee shirt to feel his abs and tight obliques. Her fingernails dug into the small of Lark's back, just enough to pull him closer to her, and she lifted her wrists to signal that she was about to either pull his shirt over his head or rip that fucker right off.

Lark stood back, raising his toned arms as Vin lifted his shirt up, revealing his smooth, muscular chest. She threw the shirt over her shoulder, not giving a shit where it landed, and Lark scooped her up, his hands grasping the backs of her thighs. She wrapped her legs around his waist, and he carried her through the living room and right into his bedroom.

As they approached his king-size bed, Lark turned around and sat down on the mattress, so that Vin was straddling his hips. She enjoyed that position particularly, because she felt like she had the upper hand; and, as she pushed Lark backwards, telling him to lie down, she felt his huge dick harden against her vagina.

They continued to make out for a couple minutes before the rest of their clothes were tossed to the side and they were both in only their underwear. Lark pulled Vin's bra cups down just enough to reveal her nipples and began to lick them firmly as he slid the straps off her shoulders. Vin lifted herself up, reaching around to unhook her bra, and Lark easily removed it. She lay back down, signaling for him to continue caressing her, however he wanted.

And boy, did he. What started with Lark's hands, tongue and lips all over her breasts quickly moved south to her belly button, and Vin lifted her hips so he could slip off her panties. He continued to use his fingers and tongue to pleasure her to heights she hadn't ever reached before. Vin's whole body shook with invigoration as she came all over his fingers.

She sighed with a deep moan, which Lark quickly took as an order to tear his boxers off and slide his nine-inch cock inside her. For over thirty minutes, they rolled around his sheets, changing positions and pleasuring each other with every deep penetration. Finally, Lark let out what seemed to be a long-awaited climax that Vin felt deep inside her, physically— and emotionally.

Panting with relief, the pair lay there in silence for a few minutes. Vin felt her eyes getting heavy; and she wondered if he was going to let her sleep there, or if he was going to simply say "thanks for the sex" and imply that their time was over and she should leave.

X X X

Vin woke up the next morning at 6:00 AM, still naked, and felt the warmth of Lark's body next to hers. She didn't want to wake him, so she quietly and carefully rolled over to plant her feet on the floor, needing to locate her clothes, get dressed and leave. This was to be the mystery that would leave Lark hanging — and, hopefully, wanting more.

As Vin took the shameful stride back to the loft, she sent Myer a text that simply read "victory."

Chapter Twenty
See You Later
April 7, 2022

Feeling a bit sluggish, Vin decided to crawl into the bed that Lark had likely slept in for years to go back to sleep. After all, it had been a long 24 hours with the flight from LA to NYC, a bit of jet lag, anxiety, alcohol, steamy sex and an underlying mission from what felt like hell.

X X X

By 9:00 AM, she was wide awake. She checked her phone to see a few missed notifications. One was from Lark, and another was from Sage. Sage had asked how she was doing, to which Vin shot back a generic "thanks girl, I'm good!" reply. She checked that one first, out of the need for some self-inflicted anticipation — she *was* super curious to find out what Lark would have to say after she'd left his place in ghost mode.

Vin tapped back to the main messages screen, seeing a preview of Lark's text. The only words visible, before she opened it, were:

What the hell happened to you? Did you just ...

They piqued her interest enough to not click on it. She needed to keep her wits about her — and she knew if she read the entire message, she would want to reply right away. What anticipation would that create for him? Absolutely none.

And so, Vin refrained, deciding to go about her morning completely ignoring Lark's text.

She headed into the bathroom, just steps away, and grabbed a towel from the cabinet under the sink. She took a quick shower, while the coffee was brewing in the kitchen, and washed her face thoroughly, revealing the few sun-kissed skin spots and freckles she'd acquired in her late twenties.

Anxiety rode through Vin's body. She'd purposely ignored Lark's attempt to reach out; but it gave her a weird sense of accomplishment, or superiority, that she had made the decision to blow him off. She ran a towel over her wet hair and began to dry and style it.

What if he knows? she thought. But how could he? Why was she being paranoid about this shit? Larkland was, legitimately, a target, nothing more than that. For her, for Myer — for everyone.

Poor guy.

Vin felt bad for him in that moment. She started to question herself and everything she was putting Lark through.

But what if he isn't a good person?

Hmmm. That thought *had* entered her mind a few times already. He sure was quick to get her on top of his dick... What if he was just as screwed up as Vin was, as Myer was — or worse?

But the chemistry Vin felt with him was way too real. She pushed aside those doubts as she walked back into the main area of the loft. Her phone was still perched on the bed charging, and she grabbed it while still wrapped in the towel.

Finally, roughly an hour after Lark's original text, she clicked on it.

What happened to you? Did you just wake up and bail on me? I was kinda wanting some morning cuddles with this hot ass actress I just hooked up with.

Well, holy shit. He just laid all that out on the line with none of the smitten, sweet charm she was used to from would-be suitors. It was honestly a bit of a turn on. Vin always dug that straight-up, straightforward shit.

Ugh, she thought. She was *so screwed.* She had to reply with something to keep him intrigued; but she also had to remember that she was on a mission from Myer, with a literal damn job to pull off.

Vin contemplated for a few moments before sending what she hoped was the perfect response, trying to make sure he was still fascinated by her.

Ha, yeah sorry just wanted to let you sleep because you looked so peaceful. Was feeling restless.

Not even a minute later, a reply.

Restless, eh? Should've jumped back on top of my dick then. Woulda been a great way to wake up.

Wow, what the eff, Lark?

He was really working it. And hell to the yeah was it working. Vin instantly felt a throbbing sensation in her pussy at the idea of waking up next to him on a regular basis to ride his smoking-hot cock.

Regular basis? This was only a one-day fling at this point — and it was set up by someone who was blackmailing her. How the hell could it ever be anything more?

Get a grip, girl. You have to check yourself.

So, she did.

Maybe I will see you later, Vin typed back.
She might as well have given him irrefutable evidence of her attraction to him — given him pretty much everything — but she had to keep up the act. Let Lark

think he'd seen all of her while keeping all that crazy shit inside under lock and key.

It was probably for the best, anyway. Even she couldn't hope to dissect that crap.

X X X

Vin desperately needed a New York famous cheesesteak, so she ventured out to grab her favorite delicious sandwich from a street vendor. Sitting on a bench just outside the new World Trade Center, she recalled the tragic events that unfolded, literally before her eyes, at that spot around twenty-one years prior.

That's, like, an-entire-person-old-enough-to-drink ago.

The temperature was a balmy forty-five degrees, kind of a pleasant contrast to the piping-hot, meat-and-cheese-laden prize in her hands. Vin took her time to enjoy her meal, her parka keeping out the chill as she soaked in the sights and sounds of the city.
As she swallowed the last bite, she felt the urge to text Lark. Just something short, something semi-neutral, she reasoned. What harm could it do?

Hope your day is going as fantastic as your night last night.

A few minutes later, Vin got up and started to head towards Central Park. In her opinion, all of Manhattan was walking distance, if you only had the discipline. She'd shoved her phone in her back pocket; so, when she felt it vibrate, she reached around for it.

Uh hell no, nothing will beat last night. Or will it? Prove me wrong?

Vin smirked.

Is that an invitation?

Take it however you want it. Literally and physically.

Oh, for crying out loud. Vin took a breath, a few moments to collect herself before she replied to him.

You have work to do here, she reminded herself. *You have to push those hormones aside and get what you came here to get ... Yeah, orgasms are great — and you are gonna get a few of those, for sure — but you have a manuscript to get, too, bitch.*

Not wanting to seem too keen and imply she'd go straight back to his place, Vin suggested they meet at a nearby speakeasy later on that day.

Lark agreed in seconds.

All set to see him again, and presumably have another porn-worthy, award-winning romp session, Vin went back to the loft to get ready to meet him at 7:00 PM.

Chapter Twenty-One
Notes
April 7, 2022

Their night out was pretty damn fun. Usually, Vin would have considered this a total win, since she and Lark were actually hitting it off quite well; but the fact that she had to keep on acting, even though she had some legitimate feelings for this guy, kind of took the shine off it.

10:00 PM rolled around, and it was time for Vin make a decision. It wasn't exactly a hard one — really, having the loft rented out felt pointless when she knew exactly where she'd end up. But it wasn't on her dime, so she really didn't give a shit.

X X X

When they strolled into his place, Lark instantly scooped her up, grabbing her ass with both hands and wrapping her around him. No obligatory drink-before-sex bullshit, not this time.

He carried Vin off to the living room, to the custom-made, oversized plethora of comfort that constituted his couch, and lay down, pulling her on top of him.

X X X

The sheer amount of orgasms Vin had on that couch, as they engaged in an hour-long session of dick-sucking, pussy-licking, and cock-thrusting, was likely record-breaking.

When Lark finally stood up, his naked body gleaming with a light sweat, Vin inspected every inch of him as the light from the next room shone over his tanned skin. She noticed a birthmark on his left ass cheek: a light-brown marking that was shaped a little bit like a heart.

Lark bent down to grab his clothes. As he straightened, Vin couldn't help looking directly at his perfect, soaking-wet dick that was still nearly hard as a rock.

"Mmmm."

"Like what you see, huh?" Lark turned towards her, put his hand around the base of his cock and began to stroke.

Is this guy for real? Vin thought, with a shiver of excitement. *What is this, Fuckfest 2022?*

It was like something straight out of a porno, the way he walked over, grabbed her face — gently — under her chin, and slowly inserted himself into her mouth.

"Taste that?" Lark asked as Vin let out continuous moans of enjoyment. "That's us, us together: like a piece of art you can't only see, but feel, smell and taste, too."

To come up with some shit like that, while her lips were around his dick, which was drenched in her cum as well as his own ... Yeah, this dude was definitely a writer.

X X X

Vin laid on the couch, completely spent, and Lark moved to the bedroom. After two amazing orgasms, exhaustion had set in, and he'd decided he'd better get some sleep.

Not Vin, though.

She waited a good thirty minutes; and, when she finally heard his loud-ass snoring, it might as well have been a shotgun to start.

In just her shirt and panties, Vin crept through the living room, past the bedroom door and into the next room: Lark's office. As she peeked in, she saw his MacBook perched on his desk, a dim light from the screen reflecting against the blinds.

It was plugged in, and it was open.

Thank God.

The hardwood floor creaked beneath Vin's feet as she tiptoed to the area rug. This was one act she absolutely did *not* need to get caught in. As she planted her feet on the soft material, with her hips pressed against the outer edge of the desk, she stopped for a second. Listened — and, sure enough, heard another loud snore from the bedroom.

Lark's apartment was a classic eight-room style one, with three bedrooms, an office, and a dining room, living room, kitchen and library. There was a lot to discover in this 1600-square-foot mancave.

Judging by the intensity of their sex-fest, it seemed pretty unlikely that Lark would wake up anytime soon; but Vin was prepared to tell him that she was just restless and wanted to walk around a bit, just in case. She also couldn't imagine he would question her, or her intentions, if she were sitting in his office taking a look at his work. But just as she leaned over to get a quick view of the screen, she felt uneasy. As if someone was watching her.

Vin looked all around. She didn't see anyone, so she brushed off the weird feeling and kept on track with her mission.

Lark's desk was completely free of any clutter, which made it easy for her to hoist her hips up and sit on it as she whisked his laptop around so she could begin to search. His Notes app was obviously the last one he'd had opened. She saw countless scribbles in a single memo, all titled like chapters. Was that it? *Was that where he wrote his manuscript, in a Notes app?* She clicked on another memo.

Nope. That one was a to-do list.

Another one, which turned out to be a bullet-point list of grocery items. As she squinted at it, Vin saw that it was a shared note. With whom would he share this list? It seemed odd. Maybe he had a personal shopper?

Whatever. That's not what I came for.

Aha! There it was, below the grocery list — "Book Notes". Vin read through them swiftly, starting to devise a plan for snagging them.

Oh my God. I forgot my thumb drive! Shit, shoot, shit!

She had to think fast. Maybe she'd just ask him if she could check her email in the morning? Shit, no: she could do that on her phone. But what if, say, her phone was dead? That was easy enough to fake.

Would she be able to copy and paste that note and email it to herself without him knowing, though? What if Lark were smart enough to go through his system operations and review every keystroke and action taken? She had to be strategic, here …

Okay: right now, this is a good start. You found his book notes. Go lie next to him and go to sleep. Turn your

phone off so you're ready to lie in the morning. You'll
probably make more headway with his permission to use
his laptop, anyway. And your head will be clearer, too.
Go, Vin, go to bed.

But Vin's nerves were too insanely wrecked to fall
asleep. She laid next to Lark, wide awake, for over an
hour, trying to come up with a sure-fire way to get this
goddamn manuscript for Myer.

Chapter Twenty-Two
Vacation
April 7-8, 2022

"Good morning, handsome," Mary muttered from her soft, plump lips as she kissed Brad's neck to awaken him. The sunlight had just started to peek through the blinds in the small apartment nestled in Little Armenia.

Brad groaned and turned over to face her, grinning.

"Honey, come on. It's time to get going!" Mary told him.

He reached over and placed his arm around her waist, hugging her tightly before playfully wrestling her with his hands.

"Brad, stop!" she demanded, through giggles, as he tickled her. "I don't want to miss our flight."

The two were about to fly to Cabo for a long weekend to celebrate Brad's record deal. Mary could not have been more excited to spend several days alone with him on their first real vacation together. They'd only been dating for a couple months, but she was unbelievably smitten with him.

No, she thought. *I'm in love with him.*

Brad stood about five foot ten and had a thin build, yet he was toned and rather lean. His hair was a dark, dirty blonde, and he was always clean-shaven despite the expectations of the country music industry. He'd always had a guitar in his hand from the time he was big enough to hold one on his own — a piece of trivia that Mary found impossibly adorable.

Mary had spent a few years dating while interning for a casting agency in Seattle, where she'd landed a position right out of college; but nothing could ever compare to the way she felt with Brad. All of those prior relationships might as well have been nothing more than long-term one-night stands.

She'd been working as an executive assistant to Myer for about a year. When she told Myer about Brad's recent success, he offered to gift her his unused timeshare points in Mexico, since he hadn't been able to use them due to the COVID-19 pandemic.

Of course, Mary graciously accepted. She couldn't wait to whisk Brad away to a world of sunshine, beaches and parties to show him how proud she was of him.

X X X

The flight touched down at Cabo San Lucas at the stroke of noon on Thursday. They rushed to their resort to check in, snag a welcome drink, and settle into their oceanfront cabana suite.

"Holy shit!" Brad exclaimed as he stepped through the glass double doors. "This place is just – unreal. I can't believe Myer just let you have it for the weekend!"

"Yep!" Mary shook her head, smiling. "He's a pretty awesome boss."

X X X

After an hour of steamy, afternoon vacation sex, featuring several orgasms and a sweaty grand finale by

Brad, they lay in the sheets: cooling off, panting, and both grinning ear to ear without saying a word.

It was nothing more than sexual success that propelled Mary and Brad to finally leap out of bed and swap their nakedness for beachwear. As they headed out through the lobby, the concierge caught them and asked if they needed any recommendations for places to go or things to do.

"Sure, that would be awesome!" Brad replied. "I've heard there are some great, romantic — and private — beaches. Can you tell us about those?"

They gathered up about as much information as they'd need to plan out a few days of adventure combined with some couples-themed activities. And, after a long day spent exploring the town and its surrounding beaches, they returned to their suite not long past sunset.

X X X

Mary was awakened by a text from Vinsetta early on Friday morning.

Hey, I already let Myer know but the last 2 days are major victory. Will fill you in later.

Mary wasn't in the mood, or mindset, to reply to anything work- or shady-plot-related. So, she rolled back over, laid her head on Brad's chest, and fell back asleep for a couple of hours.

Chapter Twenty-Three
Let's Get Outta Here
April 8, 2022

Mary properly woke up around 10:00 AM, opening her brown eyes to stare up at the large, colorful beams crisscrossing the cabana's sixteen-foot-high ceilings. She felt Brad's hand touch her side, just above her panty line, as he leaned over to her and softly whispered the three words she'd been waiting to hear him say almost since their second date.

"I love you."

Mary beamed, wrapping her arms around him, letting Brad know that she loved him, too.

Brad lightly took hold of her baby-blue camisole straps, pulling them aside, down her shoulders, and eventually past her wrists and hands so that it was merely around her waist. Mary giggled as his kisses tickled her collarbone. Brad moved his head down her navel and tugged her G-string down her hips with his teeth. His hands reached back up to grab her tits and rub his fingers over her nipples. As Mary spread her legs open for him, he began to swirl his tongue in circles over her pussy, and she let out loud cries of enjoyment.

When Brad, at last, brought his lips back up to Mary's mouth, he kissed her passionately and whispered, "I have something planned for us today."

Mary was sure she'd gone pink with excitement, and not just the sexual kind.

"Oh?" She barely uttered it in the form of a question as Brad slipped his dick inside her.

"Ohhhhh!"

Mary forgot all about her question, too absorbed by the sensation of Brad's rock-hard, wet cock sliding in and out of her, her own passionate, continued whimpers of "oh" every time he hit her G-spot. Brad made love to her for over ten minutes, his eyes never leaving hers.

For two months, they'd been having wild, animal sex, characterized by what Mary described as "shades of grey". But this — this was different. It *felt* different. Even though she hadn't said those three little words back to him, there was no way he could fail to translate her moans.

As soon as Brad exploded inside her, he let out a huge sigh. He relaxed on top of her, face pressed to her neck, breath hissing softly in her ear.

Mary ran her fingers through his sweat-soaked hair. Gripping it from underneath, with strands locked between each finger, she pulled his head up so their eyes met.

"I love you, too," she said.

They emerged from the tangled sheets moments later, abandoning their phones on the nightstand as they got dressed and moved into the kitchen. As Brad poured the champagne and orange juice, for delicious morning mimosas, into a small growler over the eat-in kitchen bar, he looked at Mary with mischief in his eyes.

"Wanna get out of here?" he asked.

"And go where?" Mary visibly perked up, grinning.

"On an adventure, with me. Just us two."

With stars in her eyes, Mary leaned over and kissed his cheek. "I'd go anywhere with you, babe."

Chapter Twenty-Four
Just Charge
April 8, 2022

The sheets began to rustle as Lark groaned. He yawned a "good morning" at Vin, his handsome face lit up with a look of huge delight.

He reached across the gap between them and pulled Vin towards him to lie on his chest. Admittedly, she was excited to be there with him in the intimacy of that not-so-fresh, morning-after scenario. Could it mean they were developing some feelings that she could later use as ammunition?

Hmm. Possibly.

"Happy Friday," Vin mumbled under her breath.

They lay in silence for about five minutes before Lark stretched his arms above his head and sighed.

"Care for some breakfast?" he asked.

"Hell yeah, sounds amazing."

Lark reached over and grabbed his phone to open DoorDash, checking what was available for delivery. His grocery list mustn't have been fulfilled if he didn't have eggs, bacon and toast in the kitchen. Vin pondered if she should hint about that to him, to see if he would fess up to the shared note. Then she would know for certain what that was all about.

"Do we need food delivered?" she asked eventually. "I'm fine with whatever you might have here."

"My grocery shopper is out of town this week for his mom's birthday, so I don't have much," Lark replied.

"You have a shopper?" Vin scrunched her eyebrows in curiosity.

"Yeah. I pay him under the table to take care of that stuff for me. I don't like using Instacart or whatever: they don't know what I want if something needs to be substituted. This kid I hired knows me — he's been interning at a publishing house. He's a sharp guy; and he needs the extra cash, anyway."

Oh, okay, Lark. Now you're showing me you have a damn heart? And here I was thinking you were just some uppity snob.

What the hell was she going to do with this guy? All she'd managed to do was learn that he was a shit-hot, successful snack, with a heart of gold and a swoon-worthy, sweet-and-spicy romance style to top it off.

Don't fall for him, Vin.

A tall order, when he was proving to be everything she'd ever wanted in a man.

As she heard the *cha-ching* of the order confirmation, Lark threw his phone back on the nightstand and said, "Thirty-five minutes. What can we do to kill that time?"

Vin felt his hand slide into her panties, and he began to softly rub her clit. She relaxed her body into the mattress, arching her back, spreading her legs open as he fingered her until she came.

Promptly after her hair-raising orgasm, Vin sat up to lean over to him and return the favor.

"How do you want it?" she asked in a whisper.

Lark grabbed her firmly — and started tickling her. "That was just for you."

He had her laughing for what seemed like a lifetime before she shrugged her shoulders upwards and jumped out of bed. She turned to him, panties soaking wet, and winked.

"I have some boxers you can wear if you want," Lark called as she went to fetch her jeans.

Well, *that* sounded seriously awesome, and comfy, so she returned to the bedroom as he pulled a pair of plaid boxers from his dresser drawer and handed them over. She slid her panties down to her ankles and between her feet and kicked them up into her hands.

It felt so damn right.

X X X

Twenty minutes later, breakfast was on the kitchen
island, and they were chomping away at delicious cheese
omelets, bacon and French toast. Lark asked her what
was on her agenda for that Friday.

Given the fact that this entire trip was a secret mission to
steal from him, Vin certainly couldn't tell him what her
real plan was. But it did seem like the perfect time to grab
her phone and *realize it was dead.*

"Hmm." Vin thought as she chewed. "I need to look at
my calendar. I think my agent has a couple virtual
meetings set up for me later on."

She made her way back to the living room, where she'd
left her phone the night before.

"Shit, my phone died," she said after a few moments.

Vin sat back down to keep eating, acting like it was no
big deal. "Maybe, after breakfast, I can log in to my
email on your computer? Would that be okay? Just need
to confirm I don't need to rush out of here."

Of course, she was on East Coast time, and there'd be no way in hell any meeting would occur before noon Eastern time. Still, it seemed like a perfectly legit request.

Just as she thought this plan was going to work like a charm, Lark leaned over to grab the charger cord that was next to the island.

"Here, you can plug in your phone."

Mother shitcrap. There went that plan.

Vin grinned as she popped the end of the cable into the charger port, setting her phone face-down on the island. "Thanks! You're a real lifesaver."

Don't panic. Just wait a few minutes, open your Calendar app, and tell a couple white lies.

She had to find a way out of his apartment — there was serious re-plotting to do. But she also needed him to know that her late afternoon and evening were open. That way, they could spend more time together. With the way things were going between them, Vin was pretty confident he'd ask her to.

150

"Looks like I have a meeting at 1:00 PM, and that's it," she said when she scooped up her phone. "I thought I had a couple meetings today, but, yeah, one got rescheduled for next week."

"Cool!" Lark said. "I'm going to my friend's comedy show tonight."

"Oh, that sounds fun!"

"Yeah, I'm meeting a few other buddies there, too. It's over in the Grid Iron area."

"Is he a famous comedian?" Vin asked. "Would I know him?"

"Eh, he's on the up-and-up. His name is Dirk Howard — he's opening for Cass Mitchell. I'm sure you know that name."

"Wow!" Vin exclaimed, genuinely impressed. "That's awesome!"

Lark radiated. "If you're up for it, you can come, too. I'd love for you to meet my friends, and I'm sure Dirk can get us an extra VIP seat."

It was all too easy. Or maybe it felt easy because they had that mutual, undeniable chemistry? Vin never thought it would have been too tough to get into his head so she could accomplish her thieving mission, but she hadn't realized she was going to get into his heart, too.

She swapped back into her jeans, draped her parka over her folded arm, gave Lark a kiss and told him she'd see him later. She walked outside to discover a beautiful sixty-degree morning and decided to take the walk back to the loft nice and slow.

Chapter Twenty-Five
Wow
April 8, 2022

The day didn't exactly fly by. Every second seemed like an hour, and every hour seemed like a week. Vin had made herself some strong coffee, and even snuck in a cigarette, which she smoked inside by an open window. It felt wrong; but then again, she felt like everything was wrong, so she didn't even care.

She sat at the glass-topped dining-room table, fumbling the thumb drive in her fingers and spinning it around on the polished surface. Holding it almost convinced her that she'd magically arrive at some mega solution.

Maybe I'm overthinking everything, Vin thought. After all, she knew that what was going down in Cabo was going to result in a huge win for everyone involved. They were all just a few days away from being free of that nineteen-year-old secret, from living completely new lives. All of their futures were going to be set. She was damn sure.

Out of nowhere, it hit her. Could *Lark* be a part of that amazing future? It would certainly change the trajectory of her trip, the mission she'd been working towards succeeding on the entire time … But maybe, just maybe, this guy was the one she'd been waiting for her whole life. The proverbial missing puzzle piece. His writing style was certainly dark and twisted — perhaps his real-life mind was just as insane. If so, a slight change to the plan could go off without a hitch.

Vin shook off the feeling. She hadn't convinced Lark — yet — that she was the right girl for him. *That* would have to be her new goal, if she wanted to test his willingness to be part of the team.

She texted Sage.

Hey hey, how are things back in LA?

Hey girl, things are good as gold here, **Sage replied.** Just working for the weekend, ha! How are you? Things going good in NYC?

Yep. All good so far! Feels weird being back here but I met a guy and I think we really like each other! Like, a lot!

Oh wow, that is awesome! Probably feels really good, since it's been a while!

Understatement of the year, Sage! Vin longed to spill to her just how unreal the sex was with Lark; but she had to keep these texts fairly inconspicuous, since Sage was part of the plan, and they couldn't risk leaving any trail of evidence. Vin tried to hint just enough about her new idea so Sage would get the point.

I might have to have you meet him one day soon, it's like, going that damn good! Let's catch up on a call soon, **Vin typed.**

Oh really? Wow. That's unexpected news! Yeah for sure, let's chat tomorrow? I'm free all day.

Vin set her phone down and sighed. She'd never intended for Lark to meet anyone she knew back in LA — that had never been part of her script. But having him do so would make everything much easier; and the prospect of him being part of the plan — and, possibly, her life after this was all over — sounded so good it gave her chills.

Vin just needed to make sure there was some truly solid trust built between them. Telling Lark about *everything* would either make him run, or it would make them stronger as a pair, since she'd no longer be hiding anything from him.

In that moment, Vin had no idea how it might turn out; but she was determined to know the answer.

X X X

A few hours later, Lark texted her.

Hey beautiful, want to grab dinner before the show?

Sounds great, she wrote back. What time?

156

I will pick you up at 5:00.

Vin sort of loved how he'd just lay out a plan: no asking if the time worked, no dancing around the subject with a bunch of alternatives. It was like he was in her head. He just knew she didn't need some overly thought-out itinerary or extravagant back-and-forth. Even though she was a major Type A, she admired Lark's ability to take the reins.

See you then, she replied.

Five o'clock was just a little over an hour away, so Vin hurried to take a bath, wash and dry her hair, and put on makeup that would dazzle Lark in ways he'd never experienced before.

She hadn't wanted to look like she was trying too hard before; but now, she definitely wanted to give off that "dolled up just for him" vibe. Of course, meeting his friends for the first time was another reason to make sure she showed her best face, but she was really more interested in seeing to it that Lark wouldn't be able to tear his eyes off her all night.

She'd packed a skintight, boutique-style dress that was simple, yet sexy and elegant. Paired with the right shoes, this was the dress that would say everything her body would if it only had the ability to talk. Its subtle mint hue was the perfect match for the pink peacoat she decided to wear — an essential for the evening, since the temperature would likely be in the forties.

Feeling in a *Sex and the City* type of moment, Vin looked out the floor-to-ceiling window to see Lark below, standing by a fancy car.

He spotted her almost instantly. Their eyes met, and she saw him mouth the one word that she couldn't wait to hear emerge from his beautiful lips.

Wow.

Chapter Twenty-Six
White Carnation
April 8, 2022

Vin went down to meet Lark, greeting him with a hug and a kiss on the cheek just as he revealed a single flower that he had obviously been holding behind his back.

"A white carnation?" Vin asked with a grin, tilting her head.

"Of course, Vin. I already know you well enough to have figured out that a rose is too cliché for you. But I also know you believe in the beauty of the simple, underestimated things in life."

What the fuck? He's so right! Vin had always loved the less showy types of flowers, dandelions being one of her favorites. She reckoned the funny-looking, bright-yellow blossoms were pretty in their own way — definitely not deserving of being labeled an ugly weed.

"Wow ..." Vin turned the carnation over in her hands and smiled. "Well, thank you."

"The rest of them are in a vase back at my place, since I had to buy a bunch." Lark chuckled.

Vin returned his laughter as he placed his hand on the small of her back and ushered her into the Uber Black he'd ordered.

As she sat next to him on the back seat, she asked Lark to fill her in on who she'd be meeting later that evening. Lark told her all about the two couples — people he'd first encountered a few years back at a benefit event — and an older guy who was his former next-door neighbor from his time living in the loft.

One of the couples had just gotten engaged; the other was married with two kids. The neighbor, Jeremy, was about ten years Lark's senior, but Lark swore you would never know it from his sense of humor and personality. Perhaps it was because Jeremy was a big-shot creative director at an advertising agency, so he always had to be witty and clever.

"Well, I'm excited to meet them all tonight," Vin said, straightening her dress.

"They're excited to meet you, too."

So, he'd at least tipped them off that he was bringing a date. But to what degree had he filled them in on their two-day shenanigans?

X X X

They pulled up to the Bula Café, a swanky restaurant that had been named after a Fijian term meaning "life" or often times, "good life". As they walked in, the maître d' welcomed Lark as if he were an old friend, with a handshake that naturally leaned into a hug.

"How've you been, my man?" he asked Lark as they separated.

"Never been better!" Lark replied, reaching over to take Vin's hand, smiling at her. Vin clasped his fingers with her own, projecting confidence with a huge grin of her own.

"I have your table ready," the maître d' announced. "This way."

The two followed him, still hand-in-hand, to a quiet little table near the back of the restaurant. Vin immediately noticed a lit candle inside a filigree-style holder and a small vase with three red roses.

"Enjoy your dinner, Lark," the maître d' said as he pulled Vin's chair out for her.

Once he'd gone, Lark turned to the table and laughed out loud. "Sorry about the roses. I had nothing to do with it."

"I'm sure most people enjoy them," She giggled.

"Of course. Whatever society says is beautiful must be beautiful, right?"

Lark ordered a bottle of wine, and they delved right into getting to know more about each other. Lark shared stories of past lovers and his childhood; and Vin even told him about her experience on 9/11 experience, when she'd lived just near the towers. Tears came into Lark's eyes as she spoke.

"Where were you when it all happened — if you don't mind me asking?" Vin said.

"I was in high school, back in Virginia. A senior."

Lark went on and on about his recollection of that horrific day, which most people could always recite like it was yesterday; and Vin felt her own eyes welt up with more than a couple tears.

X X X

Almost before Vin knew it, they were heading over to the comedy club to meet up with Lark's friends. The tone would surely change once they'd arrive, and she was more than ready to switch up the atmosphere a bit.

The taxi dropped them off at the front door, where a long line of people gathered in anticipation of snagging last-minute seats for the famous headliner. Cass Mitchell had his own Netflix series and had been touring the world for a couple of years before the pandemic hit. Only recently had he announced a new batch of live shows; so, of course, his fans were anxiously waiting to see him again.

The usher greeted Vin and Lark and released the stanchion to let them enter, confirming that Lark's friends were already inside. Vin and Lark had VIP tickets, but there seemed to be no need to show those to the usher. Clearly, he knew exactly who Lark was.

It was dimly lit inside as they walked through the lobby.

"Heyyy!" Lark shouted as they approached a group of four people sitting at the bar.

"What's up, man? So good to see ya!" The brown skinned guy on the left leaned over, embracing Lark in a bromance fashion. The other man and two women quickly followed suit.

"Good to get out, huh?" Lark asked.

"Hell yeah, man," the same guy said. "Those kids are driving us wild!" He nudged his wife, who nodded and laughed in total agreement.

Lark beamed — and, for the second time that night, took Vin's hand.

"Guys, this is my girl, Vinsetta."

Wait, what? I'm his girl? Not girlfriend, but still ... his girl?

"Hey, nice to meet you guys!" Vin said breezily, managing to keep her composure.

Lark pointed to each of his friends, introducing them to her.

"Where's Jeremy?" Lark asked, just as another man laid a hand on the back of his neck. He spun around, breaking away from Vin to hug Jeremy. "He-heyyy, dude, glad you could make it!"

"Man, I need this night out so fucking bad," Jeremy told the group. "Work is killing me. I just finished the new — hey, man, scotch on the rocks, please — sorry, that new ear pod company's campaign."

Vin stepped up to the bar to place her own order.

"Hi — yeah, two Stellas, please." Both the couples had drinks in hand already, so she figured they were likely all set. When the bartender passed the beers over, she gave one to Lark, who shot her a smile of thanks.

X X X

The seven of them chatted it up a bit before heading down the aisle to their front-row seats. It was evident they were all pretty tight friends, and Vin didn't skip a beat to make sure she'd fit right in. They even asked her about her acting career, and complimented her on a few movies she'd starred in.

Throughout the entire show, Lark never once let up from touching her, somehow, some way. He laughed almost constantly during Dirk's opening set, flashing that gorgeous smile of his in Vin's direction every so often, almost as if he was looking to her for reassurance that his friend was, in fact, funny. And, as much as Vin was enjoying the comedians' skits and jokes, she was equally enthralled by Lark and his never-ending attention to her.

During a brief lull in the on-stage action, Vin glanced in Lark's direction. He happened to look over at the same moment; and she realized, almost instantly, what was going on.

She had him right where she wanted him.

Chapter Twenty-Seven
Cheesecake
April 8, 2022

They arrived back to Lark's place several hours later; and, of course, had more mind-blowing sex. Afterwards, he walked Vin into the kitchen, his naked body leading hers towards the white carnation-filled vase on the island.

"I bought us cheesecake," he said, letting go of her and stepping over to the refrigerator. "It's from Junior's."

Ah, dangit. Junior's was, hands-down, the best damn cheesecake: not only in New York, but in the world.

Lark pulled out three huge slices and said, "Let's do dessert on dessert, yeah?"

He handed Vin a fork, and she didn't hesitate to grab a piece of the strawberry-covered delight from his hands and dig right in. As she tasted that sweet treasure of creamy deliciousness, she couldn't help but ask him:

"What's with all this special treatment? Flowers? Dessert?"

"Vin ..." Lark set the cake down, ran a hand through his disheveled hair. "You're more than I expected. I'm ... puzzled by you."

Vin smirked as she pulled the fork from her lips, leaving traces of creamy goodness behind. "Oh?"

"I mean, shit, where did you come from? You're just ... just ..." Lark paused. "You're just downright awesome. Something inside me just feels different when you're around."

Oh my God. Was it time to invite him into her completely psychologically warped plan? It had only been two days, for crying out loud! Did that even matter? She recalled a quote from a famous author she followed that stated: "time does not determine the strength of any love, it's what happens during that time that does."

An overwhelming feeling of content came over Vin. She decided, at least for now, to keep her intentions to herself and enjoy the moment of passion.

She leaned over, resting her forehead against his. Their eyes stared deep into each other's, into their souls.

"I feel the same way, Lark," she whispered.

X X X

The rest of the night was filled with flirty banter; chasing each other around; and curling up on the couch, both wearing Lark's pajamas, binge-watching a show. Vin fell asleep in his arms and awoke to him lightly kissing her forehead and leading her into his bedroom.

This time, there would be no romping — just cuddling, feeling one another's warmth, as they drifted off.

X X X

Vin woke up early the next morning, anxious that she'd been eating like a pig and hadn't worked out once (unless the multiple sexfests counted) since she'd been in NYC.

So, she quietly rolled out of bed, walked around to stand over Lark, and gently ran her fingers over his shoulder.

"Hey, handsome."

Lark made a noise that implied he was not ready to wake up.

"Is it okay if I wear your pajamas back to the loft?" she asked. "I'm going to head out and go for a run, but I don't want to put my dress on."

"Mmmmmm ..." Lark grumbled, as if leaving him alone in bed was a huge disappointment. "Yeah, babe, that's fine. Will I see you later?"

"Of course," Vin assured him as she softly kissed his lips and gathered up her belongings to head out.

She took a Lyft back to the loft. She really just wanted to get there fast instead of taking the twenty minutes to walk, to keep a momentum going and get a long run in before the day started in earnest. After all, she'd need a clear head to carry out her new plan: tell Lark everything and include him in the conspiracy.

Everything's going to plan. Lark's falling for me, which was all we, our little team, needed. Would he do anything for me? I'm not sure. But it's like the guy's under a love spell or something.

The only problem? It wasn't even a spell. Vin returned his feelings, which could well be one of the most dangerous parts of this entire plot. It wasn't even *part* of the plot. Still, though, he just *fit*.

She'd have to be careful — more than careful. With so many different cogs in motion, and knowing how shady Myer was, Vin felt a rush of paranoia. A jumble of thoughts began to take over her mind as she ran through the familiar Manhattan streets.

What if Lark already knows? What if he's just playing me?

Screw that. There was no way in hell that their connection wasn't real, and no way that Lark could have figured out anything about what she was planning to do. Myer didn't even know him. She'd been as cautious as she could.

Vin was a brilliant actress who knew when people were being genuine and when they weren't. It was a skill — one that Lark absolutely did not have in him.

Chapter Twenty-Eight
The Little Owl
April 9, 2022

Sweaty as shit from the three-mile workout, Vin snatched her phone out of the runner's waistband she had strapped on and hit the pause button on Spotify. Ironically, the song that she'd ended on was "Down with the Sickness" by Disturbed.

Ha. "Disturbed" was a damn understatement for just how messed-up her life had become. "Twisted" was more accurate, seeing as how the people involved in this madness were all intertwined somehow. And even more ironic was how seriously she was debating having Lark get involved with — well, this entire shit situation she was in.

As she panted off the newly burned calories, Vin swiped through some messages and emails from Allie. She was eager for Vin to get back to Hollywood so she could get a few pitches in front of her, mostly new casting opportunities she didn't want Vin to miss.

But in this moment, Vin was playing a much bigger role. And when all was said and done, Vin's next role was going to put her on that stupid Map to the Stars that Hollywood tourists scrambled to buy.

X X X

Vin jumped in the shower, singing the earworm of a chorus that had been stuck in her head since she'd gotten back.

"Get up, c'mon get down with the sickness … Open up your hate, and let it flow into me!"

Man, she felt kind of fucked up. She proudly reflected on the scheme she'd pulled off as a teenager — with the help of Brad, of course. She knew she did the right thing for Sage; she'd always known.

Stepping out onto the soft, memory-foam rug, Vin dried herself off from her feet up to her shoulders. With the towel semi-wrapped around her neck, she looked at herself in the mirror.

"You have an alliance here," she told herself firmly. "You have to be strong. And once he knows the truth, he's gonna fall even harder for you. Go do it. Do it *today*."

Talking to herself wasn't a foreign thing: in fact, Vin often had to do it for work, when she would recite and practice lines. This time, though, it was more of the pep talk she needed to hear, and no-one else was going to give it to her. Well, maybe Brad could, but he was off the map at the moment. And although Sage knew what was up, it was pretty early back in LA, so Vin didn't want to bother her.

Vin had already let Sage know that she planned to call her later that day. Maybe, by then, she would have integrated Lark into their story. *Maybe.* Vin had no idea if she'd even be able to get that damn manuscript, or if Lark would even take the seductress bait and agree to join her in this crazy scheme.

She got dressed in some comfortable loungewear, toasted a bagel, and drizzled honey over it. Fortunately,

Lark's loft had been stocked with some essentials prior to her arrival. She made a cup of coffee with the single-cup maker that sat on the bare countertop next to the toaster.

Looking out the massive window, at the hustle and bustle of Saturday tourists, Vin daydreamed about what the next few days would look like: for herself, Lark — the two of them, together. For Brad, for Mary, and for Sage.

Shit. It's all unfolding, finally.

She felt a bit edgy, yet also empowered.

Vin prepared a loose script in her head for just how she was going to explain everything to Lark. He would benefit tremendously from knowing it all; and, Vin reminded herself, being honest would gain his trust. In fact, the one thing she worried about was whether or not he'd be upset that she hadn't told him sooner.

Vin took a sip of her coffee. That could easily be fixed: she'd just assure Lark that she needed to make sure he wasn't being followed, first — that *she* could trust *him*. Yeah, piece of vanilla cake. She had it all planned out.

177

Sure, it probably seemed pretty shady; but he would have to understand the position she was in, right?

Right?

Vin went back to the kitchen, yanked her phone off the charger cable, and sent Lark a text.

Hope you got some good ZZZZs after I left. That run was exactly what I needed, I feel great. Ready for the day.

He didn't reply for about thirty minutes. But when he did — with plans to get together for brunch — she felt butterflies just behind her belly button.

She replied, simply, with a single word.

Perfect.

X X X

An hour and a half later, they met at a small place nearby called The Little Owl. It was at the bottom of the famous *Friends* apartment building, and it had arguably the best brunch burger in the entire city.

As Vin chomped away at a piquant cow-turned-masterpiece, she debated if now was the right time to spill the beans, or if she should wait until their post-brunch walk.

Probably best to wait. It's pretty tight in here, and the last thing I need is some squeaky fan recording us or overhearing all this crazy shit.

It was time to lay it all out and get real with him. She needed a break from the role she'd been semi-playing for the last few days; and it would only be another day or so until the news got out that Mary was missing in Cabo. She needed to save *some* of her talent to act surprised.

Chapter Twenty-Nine
Blackmail
April 9, 2022

Lark stopped dead in his tracks as soon as the words "I'm being blackmailed to steal your manuscript" left Vin's mouth.

Vin told him everything, dating all the way back to 2003; and his face never shifted, never even changed color once. Her heart thumped as she came to the end of her speech.

This is it, Vin. Whatever he does now is up to him.

"I know who Myer is," Lark confirmed. "He's a shady-ass douche."

Apparently, he'd been contacted several times by people at Pone Productions about collaborating with him, and he'd rejected their offers. He had absolutely no interest in his books being turned into movies. He was traditional that way: he wanted his words to stay only words, allowing his readers to form their own visuals from his talent.

"Oh." Guilt crept up in Vin at the thought that she'd been trying to steal from this honest man. "I had no idea," she said, shaking her head, hoping he'd pick up on her sincerity.

"What a piece of shit. Myer, I mean." Lark's head dropped a little, his neck appearing to struggle to hold it up.

"Yep. He's a major POS," Vin agreed. "So, what do you think about helping me out? We all win in this scenario."

It would mean him going against his own commitment; but now he knew everything, doing so would make him a hero in the eyes of a few — Vin's being the most important of all.

"What about Phil?" Lark asked. "How will he pay for what he did?"

"He's suffering," Vin stated. "His daughter, who he abused for almost a decade, is missing and has been for nineteen years. She's presumably dead, but they never found her body. You know that has to be killing him.

"He's offering that five-million-dollar reward because he knows what he did was so screwed up, so wrong. He will be punished one day soon, when he's in Hell. Yeah, what we did might not exactly have been ethical, but our intentions were downright moral. She didn't want to live like that anymore — she told me that herself."

Before Lark could reply, Vin felt a vibration inside her bag and pulled out an old flip phone.

"What's that?" Lark asked.

"It's my burner. Hang on, it's Brad.

"Hey, how's it going?" she answered, walking a few paces away from Lark. She didn't want him to hear the conversation, just in case it wasn't good news. Turned out, though, everything was actually great. Brad was pulling off the plan without a hitch, and he filled her in on his progress in a couple of sentences.

"Cool. Good to know," Vin said quickly. She clicked the phone's "end call" button.

She went back over to Lark, whose face was still motionless, and put her arms around him. She held him tightly, hoping that the embrace would send a spark of electricity through him, one that would damn near shock him to the point of just going along with everything she'd proposed.

"Vin," he muttered under his breath. "I just … I'm not … Are you certain this will all play out the way you've planned?"

She leaned back, arms still wrapped around him, to look directly into his eyes.

"Everything points to success. For you, for me, for us. For Brad, for Mary, for Sage. The villains here are the assholes who thought they were invincible, exempt from following the goddamn rules in this game called life. They have to pay. And we are going to *make* them pay."

"And all I have to do is hand over my manuscript?" Lark's tone was skeptical.

"Well, yes. But also, when the news breaks about my brother and Mary, tomorrow or Monday, you'll have to fly with me to Los Angeles. I think it's vital you're with me when we tell Myer that he's not the mastermind he thought he was."

Lark took a couple of minutes to digest and process it all. He took a stance that Vin hadn't seen yet, pulling back and separating his feet in a trying-to-stay-grounded sort of position. His arms crossed, and he arched his back as his eyebrows bunched inward towards each other.

"Can I trust you?"

Vin felt almost insulted; but she understood that this guy she'd been seeing for only a few days had questions. She'd just told him something that was going to either fuck his life up, or bless it, forever.

Vin stood across from him, now without any physical contact, and began to slowly tilt her head to her left. It was the start of a shake, as if to say "no".

"Right now, in this moment, I don't expect you to trust me, Lark," she said solemnly. "But I'm telling you everything because this creep *needs* to pay for what he has done, and what he is trying to do — and I want you to be part of my life on a deeper level. When we get there, on that level, you will trust me. You'll know that me telling you all of this shit was because I care. Because I want you in my life, and I don't want to deceive you. You mean a lot to me already. And you will mean a lot to some really amazing people in my life, too."

Lark didn't say anything. He didn't look at her — not directly, anyway. Vin turned slightly, following his line of sight, and saw a sticker planted on the light pole behind her. It was a drawing of a cow, only its spots were pink instead of black.

The way Lark was staring at it, she was sure his writer brain was picking up some hidden meaning that she herself was oblivious to.

Whatever it is, I just hope it makes him say "yes".

They stayed in silence for a few more moments — then, she saw something shift in Lark's eyes.

"What's going on in your mind, talk to me." She insisted with a look of concern on her face.

He pointed at the sloppily slapped up sticker and told her that a cow stood for a new beginning, and pink symbolized love of oneself *as well as others.*

No sooner than she could lift an eyebrow in shock he was that philosophical, he sternly looked at her without hesitation.

"I'm in," he said as he scooped her up into his arms.

"Let's make that asshole pay."

Chapter Thirty
Party Crashers
April 9, 2022

A few hours after Vin confessed everything to Lark, they were back at the loft. It almost felt a bit odd, since they'd only spent time together at his fancier, more affluent apartment, but Vin had asked him to come back there with her. She wanted to change things up a bit, to make sure that whatever they did together, no matter where they were, was authentic.

They'd stopped at a little brewery on their walk to celebrate their newfound partnership. By now, it was almost six o'clock, so, they were hungry for some comfort food. Lark suggested they order in some Chinese from a spot nearby that pretty much knew him by name. Vin was up for anything, given she had a slight buzz.

"Cool. What do you want?" Lark asked, pulling up the menu on his phone.

"Oh, I'm easy. Get me the sweet and sour chicken." She laughed. "Dang, Lark, I'm gonna gain ten pounds on this trip hanging around you!"

He shrugged, as it didn't matter to him what size she was: as if she'd be gorgeous in his eyes no matter what.

"Well, you'll have time later to shred this off," he said.

"Let's get to it."

Lark ordered himself the General Tso chicken, and some sides of egg and spring rolls. As they waited for the delivery, they turned on the Bluetooth speaker and danced around the kitchen-slash-living-room together to a 90s playlist on Vin's phone: laughing, bantering, and letting loose without a care in the world.

X X X

After they ate, they sat on the couch together, sipping beers and browsing through Lark's suggested shows on Netflix. Nothing seemed to spark their interest, so Vin suggested they head out to get into some innocuous mischief.

"Like what?" Lark asked.

"I don't know — let's find some stupid house party to crash or something. Why not? Let's have some fun. The next few days are going to be full of drama, and we'll need to pay a whole lot of attention."

Lark smirked. "I admit, I've never done anything like that; but I'm up for a challenge.

"You know what I used to do with my buddies when we were kids?" He laughed. "We used to toilet-paper our friends' houses. We'd take turns every weekend just getting each other back. Man, I even had this bad-ass launcher that I made."

Vin chuckled through the mouthful of beer she'd just taken.

"It would clamp the center of the roll steady, then shoot the end of the roll over the damn house," Lark went on. "It was so damn genius. All of my friends would try to steal it!"

"Too bad we don't know anyone here to toilet-paper their house," Vin said. She'd never gotten to have wild fun like that, growing up in a snobby neighborhood. It would be tough to do something like that in Manhattan, anyway, she conceded. They'd certainly get caught, for one; and two, the city was made up of only flats and apartments and townhouses.

"Okay, so I never went to college," Vin began, as they continued to swap stories about their teen years. "But, I had some close friends who I acted with in my early twenties. And Facebook, ya know, was getting heavy into photos around then. I think it was, like, 2010 or so?"

Lark gave her a look of supreme interest. "Uh-huh."

"One of them had this gargoyle statue that he'd make everyone rub on the way into his apartment, for "luck" or whatever. So, one night, my girlfriends and I stole it on our way out. We took it to a bar with us, then took photos of it with strangers all night."

"What the hell?" Lark was cracking up laughing.

"I know!" Vin snickered. "We even created a Facebook page for it and added all the photos from that night, with super-raunchy captions and shit. We sent friend requests from the gargoyle to all of our mutuals, so eventually the dude would see it. Oh my God, it was hysterical!"

"Shit, Vin, you're a trip. Tell me this was all your idea."

"Duh!" Vin rolled over and planted a big kiss on Lark's face, careful not to let the little bit of beer left in her mouth drip out.

X X X

"Let's go," Lark insisted a short while later. "Go for a walk and find something fun to get into."

"Yeah?" Vin arched an eyebrow. "Let's get the party started!"

As they semi-drunkenly pranced and skipped through the streets of Manhattan, still swapping stories of silly shit they'd done as kids or young adults, they flirted incessantly. Anyone passing by could clearly see that these two were a match made in Heaven.

It was just dusk when Vin stopped in front of a massive apartment complex near a New York college campus.

She looked up and cried, "There!" as she pointed up to what appeared to be a third-, maybe fourth-floor apartment window. "That's the party!"

Lark shrugged his shoulders. "Alright, but let's not go in empty-handed."

They mapped out the closest liquor store and stumbled in to buy a case of cheap beer to accompany their mission.

Who the hell would say no to us, walking up with twenty-four beers to split? Vin thought as she grabbed a box of Miller Lite.

"Oh my God," she shouted to Lark as she walked past the cruddy little plastic carousel that housed greeting cards. "Let's sign one of these, too!"

"Hahaha, that's so crazy it's brilliant!" Lark wrapped his arm around her waist, pulling her back towards him in such a way that she damn near got turned on in the middle of the store floor.

They paid the cashier and asked to borrow a pen, signed their names on this *Congratulations* card, and headed back toward the party.

Nearly every complex like this one had an entry system where you had to *know* who you were going to visit. Throwing caution to the wind, they busted out laughing and pushed all the buttons on the panel by the main door until they heard a buzz. They looked at each other, mouths curling upward with a mix of disbelief and triumphant, happy grins, marched through the door and strutted up the stairs.

As they planted their feet on the fourth-floor landing, the apartment door swung open and three twenty-somethings popped their heads out.

"What's up, guys? Do I know you?" One of the guys asked.

"What? For real?" Vin, ever the actress, played her part flawlessly. "We know each other from the bar." She pointed out the hallway window. "The one across the street!"

The guy pondered for a second before looking down and noticing the case of Miller Lite.

"Oh yeah!" He gave a semi-confused nod of approval, then led them right on into his shitty little apartment.

"Got you a card, my man," Lark said, handing it over. It was all Vin could do to contain her laughter.

"And beer!" she announced — not only to the kid, but to the entire party, as she swooped down and snagged it from Lark's fingers.

The whole party lit up with a loud, "Yeahhhh!"

And just like that, they were *in*.

X X X

They spent the entire night convincing all of these college kids that they were near their age, playing beer pong, flip cup and Cards Against Humanity.

Right before they left, they came clean about who they were, how they had crashed the party, as well as their real ages. Everyone laughed their asses off at their antics and thought it was hilarious.

The pair went back to Lark's place, had mind-blowing sex for two hours and passed out.

It was a fucking good night.

Chapter Thirty-One
Under Fire
April 10, 2022

Myer woke up on that beautiful, warm Sunday morning feeling as if he was on top of the world. Vinsetta had already given him the news he'd been wanting to hear: she was fast advancing to meet his demands while in New York. His forty-something-year-old body was a bit sluggish from the several glasses of Jack he'd enjoyed the previous evening, so he stumbled through his mansion to the dining room to ask for a fresh cup of coffee from his maid, Francine.

That top-of-the-world feeling began to diminish as Myer sat down on his plush, overpriced sofa and scrolled through the news app on his phone, only to learn that a young couple had been reported missing in Mexico. He clicked through to watch a video of a reporter covering the breaking story.

"A concerned staff member at the Ireland Palace resort in Cabo discovered, earlier today, that a pair of guests have not been seen since mid-day Friday. We are following developments closely as the local authorities in Mexico are investigating. The resort's security team is looking through their camera footage to identify the couple, which they hope will assist in uncovering their whereabouts."

The reporter went on to explain how the resort's cleaning ladies had found the suite in a clearly used state, and two cell phones deserted on the nightstand. All the signs pointed to the guests intending to come back, but it was evident no one had been there for a couple days.

As Myer sipped his coffee, knots formed in his stomach. The Ireland Palace was where he owned the timeshare that he'd gifted to Mary and Brad. He immediately switched over to his phone app to call Mary.

It went straight to voicemail.

"Hey, it's Mary, you know what to ..."

Myer hung up before the end of the greeting. Thoughts swirled around in his head about why she wouldn't have her phone on. Maybe they were off doing something fun, somewhere, and just didn't have service? Maybe her phone died, and she'd forgotten to pack her charger? Maybe she'd just seriously unplugged for the weekend, with no desire to have contact with anyone except her beloved Brad?

Or maybe she was in danger: hurt, missing or worse.

She knows how important Vinsetta's assignment is for me this week. She wouldn't turn her phone off.

Although Myer had been given an update from Vinsetta herself, Mary was her key point of contact for the NYC trip. Something felt very wrong.

X X X

Myer went about his day as usual: brunch with the production executives, followed by an afternoon meeting over whiskey and cigars, and all the other bullshit motions of Hollywood life. All the while, he couldn't stop thinking about the fact that his assistant might be in trouble.

By 6:00 PM, his black car was pulling back into his driveway, where he was greeted by a police officer and a gentleman in a suit. Myer rolled down the window and stared out at them.

"Mr. Pone?" asked the suited man, leaning down.

"Yes?" Myer replied.

"My name is Detective Pearson, and this is Officer Charles. Do you have a few minutes? We just need to ask you some questions."

"Sure." Myer motioned for the men to come through the gate.

They hopped back into their SUV and followed Myer's car through the gated entryway, up the drive to his front door. As they tailed him up the stairs and through the foyer, panic rose in him: the same, tied-up-guts kind that he had felt ever since that morning.

"Have a seat," Myer said, gesturing to the chairs around the massive, vintage-style oak table in his dining room.

"Can I get you anything to drink?"

"Uh, nothing for me. Pearson?" Charles asked.

"A bottle of water would be great," Pearson said.

Myer called out to Francine to ask for two bottles of water: one for Detective Pearson, and one for himself. After a couple of stiff drinks at the cigar lounge, Myer was certainly in need of it.

"Is this about Mary?" Myer asked the now-seated cops.

"I saw on the news that a couple is missing in Cabo. She was staying with her boyfriend at my timeshare there. She isn't answering any of my calls."

The two men looked at each other, then back at Myer.

"Yes," Detective Pearson confirmed. "We were contacted by the authorities in Cabo San Lucas because it appears that Mary Sipes and her boyfriend, Brad Henry, were staying in a cabana suite that you own at the Ireland Palace resort. As I'm sure you're aware of from the news reports, they haven't been seen since Friday."

"Oh my God," Myer exclaimed.

"When was the last time you heard from Mary?" Officer Charles asked.

"Thursday at 3:45 PM." Myer grabbed his phone and looked through his calls and texts to show the officers. "She texted me to let me know they had checked in, and she thanked me again."

Detective Pearson, with his chin stuck out, glared over at the screen. "Why was she thanking you?"

"I let her use my timeshare, since I hadn't been able to go there the last couple of years. It was really just going to waste."

"So the vacation was entirely on you? Neither Miss Sipes nor Mr. Henry paid you anything?"

"That's correct. Mary's boyfriend just landed a record deal and she was going to take him on vacation to celebrate, so I offered it to her."

"That's awfully nice of you, Mr. Pone." Pearson raised an eyebrow. "We looked into the ownership of that cabana as soon as we were contacted since there was no credit card on file with the resort. We did find the couple filled out a registration form when they checked in." He took out his own phone, pulling up a recent photo of the two of them together. "Can you confirm that this is Mary and Brad?"

"Yes," Myer said, without hesitation. "I think I saw that photo on her Facebook about a month ago."

"We've also noticed that Mary's life insurance policy is managed through your company, Pone Productions," Pearson pressed.

"She's an employee of mine — my executive assistant."

"Do you have any friends or acquaintances at the resort, or in Cabo, that we should know about? Any that might have information on their whereabouts?" Charles asked.

"No-one that lives there permanently," Myer said. "I have several friends that I've flown down there with for long weekends in the past, but I'd have to ask if any of those guys have been down there recently."

"I see. That will be all, then. Thank you for your time, Mr. Pone." Pearson stood, Charles following a moment after. "We'll be in touch when we know more."

"Should I be worried?" Myer asked.

"Not yet. We're hoping they turn up safely, that they just went off the grid for a couple of days."

Myer escorted the two cops back to the entrance. As soon as they left, he closed the door firmly, one hand on the doorknob and the other hand pressed against the thick slab of wood. He stood there for several seconds: still as a statue, frozen in shock.

Chapter Thirty-Two
A Nightmare
April 10, 2022

Vin woke up earlier than she cared to and rolled over to see that it was only 6:00 AM. She groaned in discontent, tossing her phone back up to the nightstand, only to miss and hear the *clunk* of it hitting the floor.

She didn't even give a shit. Her makeup was still half on her face: the rest, she was sure, was all over Lark's pillowcase.

He hadn't even budged, apparently still reveling in the post-coitus pass-out. She wondered, as she burrowed back into the pillow, if even an earthquake would shake him from his slumber.

Vin's eyes were heavy, but they also felt weirdly light. Almost as if sleep was a luxury, not a necessity. She tossed and turned; tried taking deep breaths, running snatches of some barely remembered meditation workshop over in her head.

Ugh. Sleep is not *a privilege, for crying out loud.*

Vin let out a long sigh. She was about to swing her legs over the edge of the bed, on the verge of seeing if Lark had any whisky or bourbon to knock her out, when she finally found herself back at rest.

X X X

She was eleven years old again. In a mountainous place – resembling Colorado or West Virginia. She was playing on a cheaply constructed swing set in a backyard, climbing on top of the monkey bars.

To her right, Vin noticed an elongated hill just beyond the next-door neighbor's lush backyard, which was surrounded by a metal grid style fence. She watched as a middle-aged man in a light-gray sweatsuit, wearing an 80s-style sweatband, jogged carefully down the hill.

When he reached the halfway point, a sudden electric shock blew him to pieces, scattering bloody bits of his person all over the greenery.

Despite only being a kid, Vin didn't have much of a reaction. She sat, perched on top of the monkey bars, heedless of the possibility that she could fall through them at any moment.

She stared out at the hill as another determined exercise fiend took the same path; as the woman exploded into slivers of human shrapnel that went spiraling off into the sunrise.

X X X

Vin's limbs began to jolt, and she shot awake with a huge gasp. Her chest stuttered in an out in an irregular rhythm. Her lungs felt like they were on fire.

I can't breathe. I can't breathe—

She grabbed the sheets in her fists, trying to control, to count to ten, anything to make it stop.

What a fucked-up dream. What a - ... She sighed.

Slowly, so slowly she wondered if it would ever happen, her breathing settled back into a normal pattern. She looked over at Lark, who still hadn't moved an inch, and took a deep draft of air.

It was just a nightmare, Vin. You probably just drank too much …

X X X

"Come in," she said to Lauren. "It's safe in here."

"Are you sure?" Lauren asked nervously, eyeing the abandoned shack.

"Yeah," Vin assured her, "and Brad is here, too. We're always with you; we've got your back. I promise this place is safe. Let's go."

Vin held out her hand, and Lauren followed her through the half-collapsed doorway.

Inside, every wall boasted a painting, crafted with what seemed like the entire spectrum of colors the eye was capable of perceiving. Their designs were like nothing

Vin had ever seen — nothing like those she'd seen in the art books at school. It was as if they *spoke* to her.

For a such a small shack, it seemed like there were endless hallways inside, reminiscent of a huge maze. With every turn, down every corner, there was another piece of art that struck her on a new emotional level.

At the end of one corridor, Lauren stopped suddenly. She turned to Vin and Brad, who were close behind her.

All three of them craned their necks, mesmerized by the elaborate design before them.

The hand was painted in such a way that it was reaching out to its audience. Only the palm was really visible, although there were suggestions of four fingers and a thumb, conveyed by sweeping brushstrokes. It felt comforting, familiar, yet also aggressive. What was it reaching out for? Help, perhaps? For an introduction? To hurt someone? To grab something — or maybe some*one*?

Suddenly, the colors began to run together. The hand writhed, twisted, and snapped free from the wall, the strings of paint trailing behind it cracking like whips.

Vin wasn't sure who squealed first. All she knew was they were running, running, away from the hand that was chasing them through the labyrinthine hallways, that was never less than a foot behind them.

After what felt like a year trapped on the worst haunted-house fairground ride Vin could imagine, they finally found an exit. Brad threw himself against the heavy wooden door; and, with an almighty push from Vin and Lauren together, it burst open, making the hand disappear into a colorful dust behind them.

Brad and Lauren didn't stop running. They took off down a path that led to the top of a huge hill — one that felt eerily familiar to young Vin, who'd followed close on their heels.

"NOOO!" she screamed. "No! Please, you guys, *stop!*"

Her voice had never hit an octave like that.

Chills came over Vin's body as she stood there, helplessly, watching them speeding down the slope.

"My dream isn't over yet," she said solemnly to herself.

X X X

Vin woke up before they hit that threshold where they were going to blow up into a million pieces. While that was a relief, it left her staring into space, pondering the meaning of some of the strangest, scariest dreams she'd ever had.

Chapter Thirty-Three
Pizza
April 9, 2022

It was now 9:00 AM, and Vin was all sorts of mentally screwed up.

Am I still feeling that bad about Lauren, that whole situation from damn near twenty years ago? Somewhere, maybe, deep down?

Nah, eff that. She knew she did everything right back then. She had to let it go and had to make herself forget about that insane nightmare.

Lark was still asleep, so Vin leaned over to give his chiseled, adorably hairy navel a kiss. No weird-ass horror show from her subconscious was going to mess up *their* connection.

She heard a sound come from deep in his diaphragm, like a grumble: signifying he was awake, but not quite happy to be so. It was soon joined by another noise — one that came from the floor next to the bed.

Vin turned over and reached down, pulling her phone closer to her by the charging cord. When she saw who was calling, her stomach dropped.

Myer.

The vibrations stopped just as she scooped up her phone with a roll of her eyes. Her tension eased, but only for a moment, as his number appeared again almost immediately.

"Hello?" Vin answered.

"Hey, have you heard from Mary at all the last day or two?" Myer asked in what sounded like a panic.

"Umm, I can check and see for sure. But I believe the last I heard from her was Wednesday."

"Oh, okay. Just curious."

"Why?" Vin asked. "What's up?" Her voice was still finding its normal form after just waking up, and she even yawned.

Thank God, I don't even have to try to sound clueless.

"It's just ... I haven't heard from her. That's all. She's probably just having a great time on vacation. Okay, thanks. Talk soon."

Myer hung up. Vin felt like she should have been bothered by the urgency of his three back-to-back calls, even if she did know what was really going on, but she wasn't at all.

"Who was that?" Lark asked softly.

"Oh, just that asshole back in LA, ya know."

"Cool. Everything okay?"

"Yep." Vin rolled over to lay in his arms for a few minutes. She'd have stayed there all day; but they had to get out of bed at some point to deal with their hangovers. Vin, for one, was in dire need of something insanely greasy to cure the pounding headache that had taken up rent-free residence in her skull.

Vin loved how Lark didn't question her at all. It hinted that he trusted her: much more so than other guys she'd dated in the past. They were always digging into *details* about her professional life, like how it felt to act out a love scene in a movie. That shit wasn't real — it was robotic, and any man who wasn't mature enough to understand that wasn't worth her time.

She just needed to prove to Lark that she was equally as committed, both to him and to everyone she cared about. And she was sure that, in a few days' time, she'd make that happen in a major way. After all, she was the type of girl who never let *anyone* hurt someone she loved.

X X X

They eventually rose from bed, sans sex-fest, quite possibly because they were both on the longest struggle bus ever. Vin asked Lark what he wanted for breakfast: not in a "what should we cook?" way, more of a "what can we order in — and fast?" one. She was starving.

"Pick your poison, my dear," she said as she handed over her phone with the food delivery app already open.

"Is it crazy that I really want a damn pizza?"

"Hell to the no! Let's do it."

They found a nearby pizza shop that actually had deep dish, Vin's personal favorite, on the menu. Even though she'd grown up eating the New-York-style thin crust pizza, filming a movie in Chicago in her early twenties turned her on to the rich, flavorful pie type.

"Order it all, my girl," Lark insisted with a smirk.

Vin did: one large deep dish with pepperoni, bacon and pineapple for herself, and another huge thin crust with all the meats for Lark. Meanwhile, Lark flipped on the TV and scrolled through his apps to find something for them to watch while they laid like slugs on his oversized couch, waiting for their food to arrive.

"Crime thriller?" he asked with a shrug.

"Honestly, I couldn't give less of a shit if you wanted to watch reruns of *The Nanny*," Vin laughed. She laid all the way back and stretched out as much as she could. She reached for the blanket that was draped over the back of the couch, wrapped it around her body and sighed.

Lark clicked on the first episode of a documentary series, one that delved into real-life horrors like murders, missing people, and unsolved mysteries.

"These kinds of shows really inspire me," he said as the intro sequence rolled and he snuggled closer to Vin. "Helps me convince my readers that something like what goes down in my books *could* happen, if fate created the right set of horrifying circumstances."

"I can see that." Vin laid her head on Lark's shoulder.

"I like watching old classic films, from when actors had less resources. It makes it all the more impressive when you know they're doing it without SFX and all that shit. Bette Davis? Lucy Ball? They were *real* greats."

Lark's eyes were full of admiration. He'd never given her that sort of look before, and it felt more meaningful than a simple lustful or playful glance. It felt *good,* like he truly appreciated her, just as much as she appreciated him.

"Bette Davis, huh?" he said, lifting a brow.

Mercifully, Vin's phone buzzed, and she looked over to see that the pizza delivery guy was almost here.

It was time to eat their damn hearts out.

Chapter Thirty-Four
Vinnie
April 10, 2022

After what seemed like a bottomless pizza buffet, reminiscent of setting up a souped-up version of a CiCi's restaurant in Lark's living room, they glued themselves to the crime show. Vin was in total awe of this story; and she started to really understand and resonate with what Lark had said earlier.

The victim, a girl of just eighteen years old, had been raped and brutally killed in her new apartment. The only suspect they had — who had no real connection to the actual crime — was one of her friends, a guy around the girl's age. The cops brought him in for interrogation, and it went on for days, to the point where he became damn near delusional. Eventually, he confessed.

There was just one problem: what the convicted man told the police didn't quite align with what the crime scene revealed. But that didn't matter. He went to trial, and to jail right after. The court tapes showed the victim's mother chanting that she wanted the death sentence for this horrible monster who'd murdered her baby.

It hadn't been a secret that lingering DNA evidence indicated that someone else was involved; but, since the victim's friend was assumed to be the main culprit, it had little bearing on the sentencing. However, the mother was determined to get complete justice for her daughter, and so she relentlessly, diligently continued to investigate every avenue. As it turned out — to Lark's and Vin's surprise —*she* was the one to discover that the man who'd been put away was actually innocent, and that the whole case pretty much rested on a confession made under duress.

It was inspiring to see the mother's persistence, and how she eventually became a staunch an advocate for this man who she'd originally wanted to suffer a similarly awful fate to her child. As he was set free, after eighteen years in prison, they hugged on camera.

Vin found herself tearing up a bit, and Lark even made a comment doubting if he could ever write anything that moving.

X X X

It was almost 1:00 PM when the double feature, the two-hour "holy shit, what the hell did I just watch?" stretch of time, concluded. The sun was shining through the shades that hung above the wood-framed windows.

"Ah, crap, we missed church!" Vin joked, trying to shake off a bit of the serious atmosphere.

Lark laughed and moved closer to her. He'd been a bit distant from her while they watched the show, which Vin thought was pretty understandable, given the nature of it.

"I need to ask you for a favor," Lark said as he turned to face her.

"Sure."

"I need you to be good to me."

Vin's mind immediately went on the defensive.

What has he gone through to mess him up? Who did that to him?

"Tell me, Lark," she almost demanded, "what happened to you? Who hurt you?" She took a breath, let it go. "I think we're all a little broken from some shit; but you seem guarded sometimes, and totally exposed at others. I want to know what makes you who you are."

"I was married," Lark said.

Vin was sure there was no way she'd kept the disbelief from her face, rising Hollywood star be damned. There'd been no publicity about Lark having a wife — about any relationship of his, in fact.

"Oh. What happened?" she asked with empathy.

"She and I were, well, really young. I fell in love the moment I laid eyes on her," Lark said. "She'd gone to high school with one of my new roommates, and he invited her to a big party we had planned one Saturday night."

He paused, looking off into the middle distance as if he was recalling every detail of the girl to his mind.

"She walked in — I guess she'd been driving for a couple hours — and the first thing she said to me was, 'Hi, I'm Jessie, and I really have to pee!'" Lark laughed. "I was standing there with my hand out ready to shake hers, but she just scurried right past me and my attempt to be a gentleman. From that moment, I knew. I even looked at my buddy, when I sat back down, and just said, 'She's mine.'"

"I'm guessing you got together pretty soon after?"

"Yeah. And we got married three months later, at a ridiculous courthouse. That's how badly I wanted to be with this girl forever. It was a Monday. We were nineteen."

"Wow," Vin exclaimed. "You *were* really young."

"I know." Lark sighed. "But she was my soulmate. She still is, in a way: she has a part of my heart that I'll never lease out to anyone else. I've been picky with dating ever since we signed the divorce papers. These days, it feels like so many people are really superficial or fake. Jessie was the real deal …" His gaze met Vin's again; held it. "So … Yeah, Vinnie, I worry about you. You're an actress. You play characters. That's your entire life. Are you acting with me, or is this for real?"

Shit. Shit, shit, shit. The only other person who'd ever called her that, in her entire life, was Kathy. Her biological mom. It sent a chill through Vin's body, one she hadn't felt in a long time.

"I don't like to be called Vinnie," she told Lark, her voice suddenly small.

"Oh, I'm sorry. It just kind of … rolled off my tongue naturally. I'm sorry."

"You didn't know. It's okay."

Lark continued to tell her about Jessie: how their teenage love soon broke down once they were living together, facing adult pressures. His eyes were full of sadness, and Vin could have sworn she saw tears in them when he mentioned their breakup.

She couldn't shake the feeling that an explanation was in order about why she hated the "Vinnie" nickname; and so, when Lark had concluded his story, Vin shared her own. She talked about her childhood: Kathy's abuse and psychotic episodes, all of the bullshit she had gone through as a little girl.

"I've never really told anyone all that," she said at the end. "Not even Sage, and we've known each other for years."

"Does that mean you're being vulnerable with me?" Lark asked. "Like, you trust me with all of that information?"

"Yep."

There was something about Lark that was just downright dependable. It was weird. He reminded Vin a little bit of Brad, which seemed a bit odd since Brad was her stepbrother. But she and Brad had been through a hell of a lot together, and he was pretty much her best friend. So, the fact that Lark reminded her of him wasn't necessarily a bad thing. Brad was always the type to stand up for her, stand beside her through thick and thin. He was her rock through so much shit; and, even though they hadn't become family until their early teens, they had a bond that no-one could break. Vin hoped that the same turned out to be true for her and Lark.

Chapter Thirty-Five
The Plan
April 10, 2022

While Vin didn't tell Lark about her mentally comparing him and Brad, she did tell him that she had something pretty major to take care of in a couple days.

Having him by her side for this was going to be epic. Myer was surely going to be beyond shocked. And to think that, not even a few days ago, she had no idea that she'd go from plotting to steal from Lark to falling for him …

Everything was working against Myer, going so well, just as planned. Tuesday was going to be one for the books: possibly the best day of her life, and most definitely the best day of Sage's. Vin couldn't wait.

"Remember I told you that you'd have to take a quick trip with me?" she asked Lark nonchalantly.

"Yeah. To LA, right?"

"LA. Hollywood to be exact." Vin paused. "We are going to reveal everything, and finally put Myer in his place. I think having you there with me is going to really rock his world. I mean, the guy hired me to rob you, after all."

"Yeah, that's pretty messed up," Lark said. "After what he did, I can't even imagine the pain you feel. How many years has it been, now?"

"Nineteen."

"He doesn't deserve all the fame and success he's had. It's built on pure deceit."

"I completely agree. It's past time for him to go down."

Lark stood up, stretched his arms way up over his head, and growled, "Let's get outta here."

He disappeared into his office, returning a few moments later with his MacBook. As he opened it up, Vin noticed that his file finder was open, and what appeared to be the manuscript was in the displayed folder. Oddly, it was just titled *New Book*.

Curious, Vin asked Lark if it was done or if he was still working on it. He told her that his editors were going to send back the final revisions later that week. It had already undergone two edits, line and developmental, and this last version would ensure proper formatting, punctuation and all of that fine-tuning shit.

"What about the cover?"

"It's done, too. Want to see a preview of it?"

"Hell yeah!"

Lark clicked around, pulled up an image and turned the screen in her direction.

"With One Eye Open." Vin read the title out loud as she stared at the beautiful design that accompanied it: a bright hazel eye, with subtle strokes of contrasting grays behind it, that had definitely been drawn by a talented

artist. It resembled a painting, like the ones housed in fancy museums.

"Can you tell me what it's about? Or is that a secret?" she asked Lark after she'd spent a good, solid minute admiring the cover art.

"Hmm ..."

"Well, I'm going to know soon enough, right? And *obviously* it must be out-of-this-world good, since you have Hollywood screenwriters trying to steal the damn thing."

Lark clicked back to the original folder and opened the manuscript. A dialog box popped up, prompting him to enter a password.

Interesting. It was almost as if he knew someone would try to steal it, so he'd locked it up tight. *Good thing I never tried to steal it. How the hell would I have convinced him to give me his secret code?*

"Here, read the prologue."

Vin scanned over Lark's shoulder and read the first few paragraphs. It was already proving to be as twisted and dark as his other books — possibly even moreso than what she'd experienced in her own life. Suddenly, she felt like he was meant to be on this journey with her.

"Wow." Vin looked at him with admiration. "I can't wait to be a part of this!"

X X X

They took to the internet to browse for flights to LA for the next day — the earlier the better, especially with the time zone change. Lark asked if she was just going to change her existing flight that was booked for later that week; which, of course, she couldn't do. If she did, Myer would know she was back in town, since it was booked under his account with the airline.

Watching as Lark typed in his passenger details, Vin discovered that his middle name was Joseph.

Chapter Thirty-Six
Doors
April 10, 2022

They booked flights for seven o'clock the next morning. All Vin needed to do now was return to the loft to pack up. She figured she'd bring her bags back to Lark's place for the night, since they'd be heading to the airport together.

"See you in a bit," Vin called as she headed out. Her hangover wasn't entirely cured by the greasy-ass pizza buffet, so a good long walk was definitely in order.

Myer had pre-paid for the entire week of the Airbnb stay, which meant Lark was making all that money for pretty much no reason. It felt weird, approaching those steps one last time, knowing that just five days ago she and Lark had walked up them together.

Vin stood on the sidewalk for a moment, reminiscing about that first meeting by the stoop. She pondered Lark's account of his first time seeing his ex-wife, comparing every detail of their own introduction to it like a teenage girl doodling her crush's last name behind her own. Was their initial encounter anything like what he'd with Jessie? Could Vin have possibly had the same effect on him?

As she breezed past the spot and up the stairs, Vin felt knots in her stomach. What was that feeling? Butterflies? Nerves? Hunger?

Whatever it was, she rushed to get everything together and take a quick shower, because she already couldn't wait to get back to Lark.

X X X

Just a couple hours later, Vin closed the door to Lark's old place behind her and let out a huge sigh. She ordered a ride to take her, luggage in tow, back to his apartment.

"Honey, I'm home!" she yelled jokingly as she walked in. She placed her suitcase beside Lark's dresser in the bedroom. Looked over her shoulder at the door she'd just come through.

There's just something about doors.

Vin had always felt immensely intrigued by them. She'd often look at one and wonder how many people, from how many different places, had walked through it. All the history, the baggage, of each of those people, sweeping in and out of a particular building or space.
People had been saying for years that "when one door closes, another one opens." Here she was, with the door to Lark's loft far behind her and the entrance to his home only feet away.

What was the significance? Perhaps there wasn't one for the door itself. Vin leaned a little closer to the nearby mirror to study her own eyes, the doors to her soul. She remembered a quote from one of her dad's favorite artists, Jim Morrison, of none other than The Doors: "This is the strangest life I've ever known."

In an instant, the band's famous song "The End" was playing in her head.

My only friend, the end
Of our elaborate plans, the end
Of everything that stands, the end
No safety or surprise, the end
I'll never look into your eyes again
Can you picture what will be
So limitless and free
Desperately in need of some stranger's hand

Holy shit, Vin thought. *It makes so much sense, now.*

She dashed out to tell Lark about her epiphany. Fortunately, he was also familiar with the music of the rock legends and seemed pretty inspired by her new outlook — little surprise, given his philosophical mindset.

Vin pulled out a slice of cold pizza from the box in the fridge, took a couple bites, then picked up her buzzing burner phone, which was lying next to her actual cell on the kitchen counter. It was Brad, with good news.

"It's confirmed, thank God," she said, flopping back down on the couch next to Lark. "They got the bloody blanket into Myer's office and it's in the safe. I'm so glad Mary knew the code. It's all coming together."

X X X

They stayed in that night, watched a show on Hulu and polished off the pizza leftovers with some potato chips as sustenance. The next day was going to be long as shit, and they needed to be rested up.

Chapter Thirty-Seven
Flight
April 11, 2022

The alarm went off abruptly at 4:00 AM.

How in the world they'd managed to go the entire Sunday without any sex was beyond Vin's comprehension. They had to be at the airport in an hour and a half, but still ...

She slowly slid her panties off and scooched her ass backward until it reached Lark's groin. She stretched her arm back to grab his dick, pulled it free from his boxers, and rubbed it between her ass cheeks and along the lips of her pussy. She felt herself getting wetter and wetter as his cock hardened and he began to moan in excitement.

Lark jerked his head closer to her neck, and she arched back just enough to whisper in his ear, "Put your cock inside me."

Without pause, Lark did as she said and thrusted away, harder and harder with every penetration, for just a couple minutes. That was all he had in him, which was fine with Vin since they were on a tight schedule.

"Now that's how we get a long day of travel off to a good start," she chuckled.

They hopped out of bed and took a shower together. When Vin wrapped her soapy, lathered-up arms around Lark's waist, she was astonished to discover that he was, yet again, hard as a rock.

"Hey now, what's going on here? Feels like you kinda want to sex me up again, Sir Author."

"Oh, I do," he said with a firm, bass-like tone, as if the mere fact she'd called him "Sir Author" was a turn-on.

Lark turned around and grabbed her tits, sucking on her nipples as one of his hands slid down to stroke her pussy. This time, he didn't finish, but he made sure to pleasure

Vin so insanely hard that she orgasmed twice in under a minute. Her clit had never been loved so much in such short amount of time.

X X X

They got dressed and ready to head to John F. Kennedy airport. Vin had always wondered what it would be like to fall in love with an adventurous man, to travel to exotic places with a partner in crime. This was going to give her a good taste of that ... and even though what they were about to do was criminal, she considered it a moral retaliation.

Vin really appreciated how Lark traveled lightly. Even though the guy wore a size thirteen shoe, he didn't pack five pairs and demand to bring a checked bag. Instead, he wheeled a carry-on size suitcase with his essentials and a modest amount of casual attire.

Every day that Vin got the chance to know him more, she found her attraction to him undeniably growing. Lark was totally her type, which was, weirdly, something she hadn't thought about since they'd met. In the past, she'd dated anyone who had shown her they were stand-up; but she'd never clicked with any of those guys like she did with him.

There was one other thing she really wanted to know about Lark, though her thinking of it in that moment might have been down to her being hungry more than anything else. Could he cook up a good medium-rare steak on the grill? Potatoes? Stuffed mushrooms? Corn on the cob? Did he know about the trick to add an ice cube to the aluminum wrapped around the corn ears?

She decided to just flat-out ask him.

"All of that and more!" Lark replied with a grin. "I guess I'm gonna have to make you a fantastic dinner one night soon."

Vin's eyebrows lifted, then her mouth started to water at just the thought of a night like that with Lark.

X X X

They stopped at a little airport café to grab some breakfast before the flight started boarding. Given that she'd been eating like absolute shit for the last few days, Vin opted for a healthier plate of fruit and an omelet with egg whites and bacon. A little protein would serve her well, anyway, as they embarked on their mission. Lark ordered himself a coffee and bagel with cream cheese, like an easygoing, uncomplicated guy.

"No mimosa for the lady?" Lark asked, shaking his head as if it was funny to assume they'd be drinking that early.

"Ha! Nope, not today."

X X X

Vin really wanted to nap on the flight — especially since Lark had almost immediately passed out next to her — but she knew there was no way in hell she was going to be able to get a wink of sleep. Her mind was already racing; and, at times, her heart was even pounding. They were just one day away from executing Operation Uptown Girls.

She giggled quietly to herself. *What a stupid codename. How our still-developing brains even came up with this brilliant shit, I don't know.*

X X X

Nearly five hours later, they touched down at Los Angeles International Airport. Vin had spent the entire time daydreaming about how Tuesday was going to go down. It was almost like she was manifesting the best possible outcome, like some pretentious dickhead who'd subscribed to *The Secret*.

She'd leaned her head on Lark's shoulder for the majority of the trip. When he woke up a couple hours in, he asked what he should be expecting; and Vin just told him the truth about everything that was on the agenda for that day, and how the confrontation with Myer might go down.

"Thanks for having the sense to just bring a carry-on," she said playfully as they emerged into the late-morning sunlight.

Lark shrugged. "Why wouldn't I? There's nothing worse than having to wait for eons for your bag to finally drop on that damn carousel."

Vin couldn't agree more. She was especially grateful for Lark's practicality now, since they needed to get moving. She'd already checked her burner for any missed calls or voicemails, expecting to hear from Brad about their arrangements for later that day. The flight had landed a bit early, but he knew when they'd be there.

Vin was anxious for Lark to meet him. It sucked that they had to be introduced under such stressful circumstances, but the celebrations were coming soon enough. Of that, she was certain.

Her cell phone, however, had a few notifications she couldn't ignore. Sage had texted her a couple updates, and wanted to get together for a late lunch to catch up, seeing as they'd never had the chance to gab on the phone over the weekend like they'd planned. Still, Vin knew they were on the same page. They always were.

Chapter Thirty-Eight
Disguise
April 11, 2022

With a full day of duplicitous activities planned out, they had to get to Vin's place as quickly and quietly as possible. Luckily, the taxi arrived just a few minutes after she booked it, and they were soon heading up the paved walkway to her ranch-style house.

As Vin pulled out her keys from her patchwork Burberry handbag and unlocked the door, she noticed that her porch plants were looking pretty sad.

"Aww. I was only gone a few days, guys!" she cooed. "I know you need some love, but I'll get to you later. Promise!"

"Are you … talking to your bushes?"

"Of course! It helps them stay healthy. You know, good communication is key," Vin said with a wink.

Lark laughed, slapping a hand over his face. "Do they communicate back, then?"

"They do when they grow!"

"Touché."

It was a bit drab inside, owing to Vin having closed the blinds with the shades down before she left, so she flipped the light switches to brighten up the foyer and den area.

"Ta-da! Welcome to my humble abode."

Lark blinked.

"What? Not quite your style, Sir Author?"

"It's not that," Lark assured her. "I just … I thought you'd be living in some fancy-ass mansion, you being an actress."

Vin giggled, grabbing hold of his hand and pulling him through the entryway. "We're not all a bunch of show-offs. Come on. I'll prove it."

X X X

The tour didn't take long, and soon they were sitting at the kitchen island, snacking on some veggie chips Vin had in the cupboard. Her burner phone started ringing in the front room, so she ran to pick it up.

"Flight go okay?" It was Brad. "You home, safe, good, happy?"

"Yeah, kiddo." She couldn't help but laugh at the number of questions he rattled off, though she figured he'd have a few since they hadn't talked much while she was in NYC. "Are you? You ready? You nervous?"

"All questions I can answer when I see you in a bit."

"So that's a 'yeah.' You're nervous."

Brad had always been that sort of type, but he'd come such a long way since they were kids.

She heard him take a deep breath.

"I'm actually good. We got back yesterday and got right to work. Everyone still thinks we're missing in Cabo; but, ya know, it's only been a couple days, so no one seems to be majorly freaking out just yet."

"The suspicions are definitely starting to heighten," Vin pointed out. "I got a call from Myer yesterday."

"You did, huh?"

"Yep. Concerned about Mary. Asking me if I had heard from her. I told him no: not since last week, I think Wednesday."

"Well, perfect." Brad spoke with a sudden confidence, and firmed up their plans to meet in a couple hours.

X X X

Since everyone thought she was still in NYC, Vin had to be completely under the radar. Fortunately, she had tons of shit in her wardrobe from past acting jobs that would enable her to pull off a completely different look. She even had some heavy-duty, SFX-type makeup that could render her unrecognizable.

Lark, meanwhile, might have had a shitload of fame from his books, but he'd purposely never shown his face in a photo on his publications, or even in the media much. It was unlikely that anyone would recognize him, especially out in LA. Still, Vin suggested he wear a hat, scarf and sunglasses: something a bit offbeat for his style.

As she dressed Lark up like a Ken doll, he asked, "Why didn't we have to wear disguises on the way here?"

"I thought about packing a few things to do just that before I left," Vin said, "but knowing the whole Brad-and-Mary thing would happen while I was there, I figured it'd look natural for me to fly home when the news broke. Seeing me at LAX wouldn't be unusual at all. But seeing me at Green's? That'd be sketchy, at the very least."

X X X

They ventured out again as two entirely different people. A pair of friends, as opposed to a couple; a black-haired,

Italian-looking girl, accompanied by a guy who appeared either super-metrosexual or to be leaning into that not-quite-straight stereotype.

The complex around Green's had by now been turned into a fancy lifestyle center, filled with high-end department stores, yoga studios and the like. But the restaurant that had been there for sixty or so years was still a staple — and no one was going to tear it down or replace it.

It was after the lunch rush, and there were only a few other patrons there. Not much had changed at the little joint, not even the furnishings and décor. The seats were still a bright yellow color, although a bit run-down, with some minor cracks and tears. The tabletops were exactly as she remembered: a gray-and-white, marbled slate style with silver casing.

Lark followed her inside as she headed to the first booth, closest to the door. He sat beside her, not across from her: possibly a nod to his awareness or anticipation that Brad would sit on the opposite side, once he arrived.

Vin noticed that one of the screws that held the casing onto their table was loose. She felt a strong relation to that screw, as if that old saying "she has a screw loose" all of a sudden applied to her.

To hell with that. My screw's always been tight. Always.

A waitress came and asked what they'd like to drink. Both of them ordered quickly — Lark an iced tea, and Vin a glass of water. She also went ahead and ordered Brad a Sprite, since she knew that was his go-to.

"Great! I'll bring some menus for the three of you."

"Thank you." Vin smiled at her.

Not even a minute later, Brad walked in, sporting a fedora hat, glasses and more facial hair than usual. He made the quick turn to join them at the table. Lark was sitting in the outside position, so he scooted out to stand up when Brad approached.

"Heard a lot about you. Good to meet you," Lark shook Brad's hand firmly.

"Can't say the same; but no doubt, if you're here, you're a good dude."

Vin's heart melted a little bit. Her stepbrother — her long-time accomplice — and newfound partner in crime were finally meeting!

Now, they just needed to add Sage to the mix.

Chapter Thirty-Nine
Evidence
April 11, 2022

They sat around the table for a few minutes, just shooting the shit. Lark and Brad got to know a bit about each other — never using one another's real names, of course — shared a few jokes and made some small talk. Brad had a funny way about him, with clever puns and comments, that could lure anyone in. It was a perfect lunch meeting over burgers for the guys and a Greek salad for Vin.

But, as much as she'd have loved to just enjoy the moment, they had to get down to business.

"Alright. Fill me in on the last few days," Vin demanded, looking to Brad.

"Mary is awesome, she is totally on board with everything," he said, a little sparkle in his eye. "I think she's actually stunned that she's working for such a douchebag. She really had no idea."

"Okay. Did she take care of the DNA? Blanket? The locket, hair?"

"Yep. He's totally pinned."

Lark looked back-and-forth between them, nearly pretending to know exactly what they were discussing. Vin had hinted to him about what had gone down with Brad and Mary going "missing" in Cabo, and how they were directing all of the suspicion towards Myer. They needed him to have a major distraction, so he felt nervous being a suspect for a crime, even though he didn't commit, *this* one. With that assured, they could now focus on payback for the crimes he definitely knew — and never said a word — about.

"What a coward," Lark muttered.

"Exactly." Vin slowly moved her gaze from him back to Brad. "I knew, the moment I learned what he'd done, that he'd have to be punished. What kind of person would never speak up after seeing some shit like that?"

Vin had already filled Lark in on the entire nineteen-year-old story. He'd responded with such empathy, in his face and in his entire disposition, she knew he understood why they were doing all this.

Lark's one of us, now. He's a good guy. And good guys don't like it when bad guys get away with things they shouldn't.

It was all set. The bloody blanket, the strands of hair, even a locket that Lauren's grandma gifted her that she'd always worn around her neck. All of it was planted on Myer, thanks to Mary. Since she worked as Myer's assistant, her fingerprints, or any evidence that she was in or around his office, wouldn't raise suspicions at all. Myer even granted her access to the safe he had in there, he trusted her so implicitly.

Vin sipped her water, mulling everything over. When they were fourteen years old and thought they were smart as hell, they'd planned to pin this all on Myer, but they hadn't worked out just how it would execute. They were at least clued-up enough to realize that any sloppiness could end in disaster, and so they decided to wait until they had a better plan. Or until fate played out — which, deep down, they knew it would.

Looking back, life happened. They'd become these blossoming young women that had such bright futures after the bullshit they went through as teens. And although they never forgot about their intention to, one day, take Myer down, they decided to live their lives as best as they could. Especially since they had created them to be just as they were — beautiful, fun, vibrant, carefree and purposeful.

Perhaps they just needed to grow up, and into the people they were today, in order to be *who* they needed to be to truly prepare to make all of this shit go down …

"Have you talked to Sage at all?" Vin asked her last lingering question.

"Yeah," Brad confirmed.

Vin couldn't help smirking. Sage's presence was going to be the icing on the cake — and Myer hadn't a clue.

X X X

It was almost 2:30 PM when the bell over the door rang. Vin looked over her shoulder, and Brad's chin lifted as a huge grin smeared across his face.

She recognized Mary's smile, first, beneath her jet-black, short straight wig and unusually heavy makeup. A recent meeting, to go over the details of the blackmail scheme, had made it a familiar one.

"What a trip this is, huh?" Mary said, reaching out to greet Vin with a handshake.

"Damn right." Vin elbowed Lark to move so she could give her a proper hug. "We're all in this together, now. Did you ever see this coming?"

"Unreal, girl. It's just unreal."

They embraced, chattering like teenagers who had been friends forever.

More small talk bounced around the table; then Mary started telling them about some of the weird shit that she'd have to deal with as Myer's assistant. Most of it was just kind of funny, odd demands and weird little nuances. They aligned pretty well with the typical kind of self-centered, entitled type of boss Vin felt most people had to deal with at some point in their career.

Doesn't seem like he ever had any serious intention to hurt anyone, though, she thought. *Maybe he really was in the wrong place at the wrong time — and maybe he's blackmailing me to get his own form of revenge for what he thought he saw.*

No. This was their revenge for what they *knew* he saw.

Chapter Forty
Apartment E
April 11, 2022

Vin decided Myer was still an irredeemable asshole. He'd witnessed a real crime, a violation of the highest order, and kept his mouth shut; but he was prepared to go all-in to expose a murder, both for his own selfish ends.

Their group had only loosely planned out an agenda, to avoid any technology trail of their plotting. Sure, Brad and Vin were using burner phones to communicate, but they kept that to an absolute minimum. After all, Brad was supposed to be missing.

6408 Zwickel Station, Apartment E was their first port of call. They had to do a little scoping out, considering it had been a good fifteen years since they were last there.

It was the perfect place for meeting Sage, too: she knew the building all too well, although Vin wondered if it would be a comfortable place for her.

Vin, Lark, Brad and Mary stood in the desolate parking lot adjacent to the small train-station-turned-apartment complex. With the sort of folks who lived here, Vin was confident that no-one would question who they were, mostly down to the fact that they weren't likely to give a shit unless these strangers had money or food to give.

She'd always made a point of bringing some canned goods or extra cash whenever she'd visit back in the day; but right now, she had bigger problems to focus on.

A newer-model Audi rolled up, and Vin saw Sage gazing through the backseat window. Vin shrieked in excitement, running over to throw her arms around Sage as soon as she stepped out of the car.

"Holy shit, girl, I haven't seen you since my birthday!" Vin exclaimed as Sage finished thanking the taxi driver.

"I know, I know!" Sage returned the hug with just as much enthusiasm. "I missed you so much!"

"How are you? How's Barry?"

"Things are good! He's busy with work, and I'm just trying to keep my freelancing going. I've been working on a few major projects for some agencies lately."

"Yeah?" Vin leaned back, her hands still grasping Sage's upper arms. "That's so cool. I want to hear all about all of it!"

Sage had taught herself graphic design when she was younger, and she had such a natural talent that it came easily to her. For about ten years, now, she'd been plugged into several networks, both local and national, which only the most notable designers were invited to be a part of. Los Angeles was just an amazing place to be if you were in any sort of artistic industry, and knowing the right people was more than half the battle.

"This place …" Sage gazed up at the building. "Holy shit, Vin. I can't believe we're here."

"Uh-huh. Feels weird, doesn't it?"

Nearly twenty years of secrets, and they're all about to be exposed.

The others were standing back, close to the three short cement stairs that led up to the ground-floor Apartment E. Sage and Vin went over to them, with Sage taking the time to introduce herself to Lark before saying "hello" to Brad and Mary.

"You guys look funny, but it works!" she laughed as she gave them cheek kisses and hugs. "Brad, it's been way too long since I've seen you."

"I know, right?"

Vin quickly brought the conversation back to their plan — specifically, their agenda for the next day — and she made sure to give everyone a breakdown of exactly what they should, and would, be doing, and asked all of the accomplices what they thought.

Mary described how she'd disguised herself, in a little less out-there way than her current getup, and planted all the necessary items in Myer's office after remotely disabling the security alarm and camera. The blanket, along with a couple strands of Lauren's hair, was hidden in the back of his safe. That was the smoking gun; but, just to be safe, she'd also hidden Lauren's locket in his desk drawer, behind a shitload of papers he'd likely not touched in years.

"And if he decides to take a look in that desk, especially with us 'missing,'" Mary added, "we might get his fingerprints on the necklace, which makes it all the more damning. Sure, he could find it and wonder why the hell it's there, but I'm sure he would assume it belonged to some one-night hussy he'd brought back to the office."

What Mary had done was no easy task, but she had the huge benefit of knowing exactly where Myer would be that Sunday — at the cigar lounge. True, she was his assistant, but it seemed she had a superpower of being aware of her boss' schedule even when it wasn't written down.

Brad stood there, nodding his head.

"We have to make sure Myer knows that Mary and I are more than prepared to go missing permanently," he added.

"With all that evidence already in his office, I'm willing to bet he won't want our blood on his hands, too."

Mary smiled. "Got it covered. I added a typed note on his desk, telling me that I'd regret it forever if I resigned. He's out of the office until later this week, so there's no way he'll find it before we get to him. I even added a few resumes to the pile of papers on his desk."

Brad looped his arm around Mary's waist, pulling her closer to him. He was proud that she, in fact, had it in her to be so full of wit.

Sage confirmed that she was ready; and Lark, poor guy, looked as if his head was spinning around. Vin felt a little bit bad for him, since he likely felt super out of place in an entirely new city, with people he didn't know or trust. So, she moved to stand next to him to make sure he still felt the closeness that they'd shared back in New York.

"Are you okay?" she asked him softly.

Lark's left eyebrow lifted — semi-reluctantly, she thought.

"Yeah, I think so," he said.

It didn't seem so reassuring, but Vin knew she could calm him down later and answer any questions he had —

if he had any left. She'd been pretty detailed and thorough these past couple days; but meeting the plotters in person must've been overwhelming for him.

"We *are* doing the right thing, here," Vin declared, to everyone standing in the circle. Not as though she needed to say it out loud; but, in the moment, it felt like a much-needed reassurance.

Chapter Forty-One
Two Girls
April 11, 2022

It had been at least ten years since Vin had last seen Drum. They hadn't met since a random run-in at a grocery store in the village, where he was shopping with his wife and new baby. He'd married his college sweetheart, and they were extremely happy and in love.

As such, Vin didn't have any current contact details on hand for him. But knowing Drum as well as she had done, she was willing to bet his number hadn't changed from when he was the resident drug guy at Green's.

She tapped it into her cell — no need to use the burner on this one, since she wouldn't be discussing anything overtly suspicious. She'd go in with the usual catch-up-between-friends bullshit and steer the conversation towards gauging whether he still had any association with Warwick, the guy she'd rented Apartment E from back in 2003.

If he does, we might be fucked. I can't have him putting two and two together.

Vin pressed call. It rang a few times, and her heart damn near jumped into her mouth with every break of silence.

"Hi, this is Damon. I can't take your call right now ..."

Vin breathed a sigh of relief.

"Drum, hey, it's Vinsetta!" she said after the message tone beeped. "I know it's been forever, but I was just thinking about you and wanted to say hi. Hope you and the Mrs and the kids are doing great. Give me a call if you get a chance!"

X X X

Her phone didn't buzz until the evening. When Vin reached over to pick it up, she saw a text from Drum.

Hey hey girl, long time! At dinner with the family but let's catch up soon.

Crap. At this rate, she might not be able to confirm anything for another day, or possibly longer.

Vin thought for a few moments, then typed out her reply.

Sounds good! Drove past Green's earlier and it brought back so many memories. Oh the good old days!

Hopefully, that would get him to at least hint as to whether or not he was still involved with that old crowd at all.

Holy shit, yeah! **Drum replied.** Ha! I was like such a bum back then, my God. I don't even live there anymore, I'm in Florida now. Been working here for a few years!

Boom. If he wasn't even in the area, he definitely wasn't still in communication with Warwick. Drum had always dealt with people on a face-to-face basis pretty much exclusively, considering his pretty shady, underground style of doing any type of business.

Oh wow, that's so awesome. Good for you! I'm free to catch up any time, talk soon and enjoy dinner!

She liked Drum and didn't want to be short with him; but she needed to close out the conversation and refocus her energy for the next day.

X X X

Lark was in the living room, relaxing on the couch with a beer.

"Just need to take that edge off," he said as Vin came in.

"Feels like 10:00 PM. Guess I'm just still on New York time."

As Vin walked over and stood in front of him, Lark extended his legs on either side of hers. His feet turned inward, sort of pigeon-like, and wrapped behind her calves. When he pulled, she nearly fell on top of his body.

Vin gave her best flirty laugh, despite all of her nervousness. "What are you doing?"
"Just tryna get you closer to me, beautiful."

"Only one beer in, eh?" she joked.

"Zero to a hundred, doesn't matter. Need you close."

Well, isn't that the sweetest shit ever?

Vin continued to stand over him, but she leaned down and gave as much of herself to Lark as she could without it leading to Spring Sexfest 2022 encore. She didn't have the time for it; but she also felt awkward, and a little guilty, about it, given her plans for the night and the next day's itinerary.

"Mmm ... Aww, babe," she hummed into his ear. "I just, ugh, I have to go meet Sage for a few. Is that cool with you?"

"For sure," Lark breathed, letting go of her. "Go hang with your girl."

"Yeah? Sorry, we just need to chat about some shit. Girl shit, ya know."

"No worries. There's more beer in the fridge, so I'm good."

Vin got him all set up with the streaming service remote and let him know there were plenty of options if he wanted to chill and watch a show or two.

"I won't be long," she assured him.

X X X

Vin had no plans to drink, so she drove straight out to meet up with Sage. She pulled into the parking lot of an old warehouse that had burned down a couple years ago and spotted Sage's car in the distance. She parked right beside her.

Rolling down her window, she gave Sage a joking sultry look and whistled.
"Hey, girl, hey!" she called.

Sage laughed as she shook her head. "C'mon, get in!"

Vin relocated to Sage's passenger seat and looked down at her phone to check the time. It was almost 8:00 PM.

"He should be here any minute," she said.

Sage sighed. This wasn't going to be much of a blast from the past for her. She'd dissociated with the bullshit so much that she didn't really feel like anything bad had ever happened to her. In many ways, that was a good thing. It allowed her to be the woman she probably never would have become, had she remembered everything.

A set of headlights glowed on the horizon, growing larger and brighter each second.

"That's him," Sage said, looking out of her driver-side window.

Vin nodded, trying to keep her agitation from her reply. "Let's do this."

Concurrently, they pulled the handles to open the doors that were going to lead them into this secret mission. One that no-one knew about except for these two girls.

This was so much bigger than the old Uptown Girls plan they'd drummed up as teenagers — it was born of a conviction their fully-developed, adult brains had set upon just a couple months prior.

Chapter Forty-Two
Warwick
April 11, 2022

His mid-2000s Buick rolled up right next to the two of them. Warwick was always a smooth dude who gave off a vibe that he gave zero cares about anything in the world. These days, he was easily approaching sixty years old, which meant his fuck bank was probably in the negative.

Warwick slowly stepped out of his car to hover grandly over the two of them, nearly shadowing their more petite figures. Warwick was easily six-foot-four, with pronounced dark features as if he was possibly Italian, or Middle Eastern, she never really knew for sure. Even though his exterior was a bit like a hard candy, he'd always been respectful to Vin, and especially to Sage.

Because I was a cash-paying customer who knew Drum.

This guy had always been all about the bankroll and nothing else. For that reason, there were times Vin had worried a bit about his discretion; but dabbling in potentially criminal shit cooked up by a bunch of teenagers just didn't feel like something Warwick would subscribe to. He'd always felt like *their* type of person.

It was strange to even think that they had their own type of people. But it seemed to be the way the world worked, what with social media emerging, and narcissism on the rise — almost like they were the heirs of good folks who'd be driven together by wrongdoings and made difficult, perhaps illegal, choices to avenge them, to do what was right.

"Wow, holy shit." Vin didn't even hold back how she felt.

"Warwick. How are you?"

"Girly girl, I'm good, always good."

His super-bass-toned voice was one she had nearly forgotten, but the memories snapped right back into place as soon as she heard it. And it felt like home.

"So, I'll cut to the chase here," Vin went on, "'cause I know that's how you like it."

"Always, always."

Warwick was a man of few words. In that moment, Vin wondered what it would have been like to have sex with him. Would he up his vocabulary to include something other than the same mundane phrases he'd used over the past twenty years? She couldn't but question who Warwick was beyond the cut-throat, drug-dealer type of personality he'd always boasted.

That's weird, Vin. Get on with it.

"I know I paid you handsomely for ten years of rent for that apartment, in cash," she said. "And even though we haven't occupied it for quite some time now, it's still mine. I've paid you for it through, what, 2023 now, right?"

"Yes ma'am, you're good." Warwick flashed his characteristic big smile, revealing grungy teeth that showed his age.

"Okay. I need to be better than good, though."

"What's up, girl?"

Vin glanced over at Sage, who was standing beside her with a look on her face that could have given it all away, if only Warwick knew.

"Okay, how many other tenants do you have there?" Vin asked. "Do you have another property they could move to?"

"That's a weird damn question, girl. Why?"

"I will pay you in cash, for all of their rent, for a year, as well as any other costs associated with moving them. And if you can up your insurance policy on that property quickly, that would only benefit you. Trust me."

"Heavy ask," Warwick said casually. "Lots of my people have been there forever."

"Make it happen — no questions asked, before May fifteenth. And when you do, you will be handsomely monetarily rewarded."

Vin played that card heavy, knowing Warwick would bite.

X X X

After only three or so minutes of conversation, Warwick agreed to the deal.

They all hugged a quick goodbye, and Warwick's gaze lingered on Sage for a moment.

"Was a pleasure helping you, girl," he said, his tone heartfelt. "Glad to see you in a better place now."

Sage's eyes teared up a bit. She seemed to have been recalling the near-endless days at the apartment: an experience Vin couldn't truly imagine, even though she'd made daily visits when Sage had first moved in.

Vin closed her eyes tightly, put her arm around Sage's shoulders.

"It's going to be okay. Everything's going to be okay. I promise."

As Warwick's car peeled out of the parking lot, Vin took out her burner phone and gave Brad a call.

"It's a go."

Chapter Forty-Three
A Bad Day
April 11, 2022

Brad closed the flip phone and gave Mary a quick, admiring glance. What she was about to do was going to be the highlight of the entire plot.

"Yeah?" she asked him, with a grim, curious, look on her face.

"Yep." He reached down to take her hand and pull her close to him. He wanted to touch her, to make her feel loved, so she'd feel confident in her mission that night.

"And how do we know exactly where he'll be?" Mary asked.

"Vin did her research. It's Monday. He always plays poker at a small underground joint until ten-thirty or so. This is going to be easy."

"Okay ..." Mary's tone hinted that she needed to know more. "What's the plan?"

"There's a small bar just a block from that parlor. With the neighborhood being a little sketch, I'm going to stay close by. Don't worry."

Brad was never going to leave Mary alone in any sort of dangerous situation. But knowing Phil's obsession with young girls, she was the safest bet to pull this off. Especially since Phil's wife had left him about a year prior — it had been plastered all over the news that he'd had an affair with one of his company's 18-year-old interns. Although the girl was of legal age, it didn't sit well with his peers, nor the millions of people who regularly utilized his internationally web platform.

Mary bit her lip. "I just have to walk by — like, on the street — and catch him before he gets into his car?"

"Yep," Brad said again. "Catch his eye. Talk to him. Ask him if he'd like to join you for a drink at that bar. He'll bite, no doubt."

Mary spread her fingers, resting them against her chest as she let out a heavy breath.

"I got this."

Mary went into her bedroom and pulled out her "slutty" clothes, parading a few outfits to Brad as if it was a fashion show. Soon, they were cracking up over some of the choice attire she'd actually worn out to clubs.

"What the hell is that?" Brad rolled over, cackling, as Mary strutted out in a sequined tube top, with a tulle netted skirt so short that it might as well have been just a hair tie strapped around her waist. "Please tell me you never actually wore that in public?"

"Sorry to disappoint!" Mary snorted with laughter, striking a few exaggerated poses in the full-length mirror.

Eventually, Mary pieced together the perfect late-night dress and jewelry for the mission. She hopped into the shit-ass car they'd been driving since they paid $1,000 cash for it back in Cabo, and they headed off to Hermann Street.

X X X

"I'm right here, babe," Brad said, squeezing Mary's hand as he pulled up to the curb. He turned off the lights and parked right in between the two locations, so he'd have bird's-eye view of everything that was about to go down.

Having a beat-up 2002 Chevy Impala turned out to be lifesaving: it seemed like it fit right into the neighborhood. No one would question if it belonged there.

"I know, I'm going to do great." Mary leaned over and kissed him, then stepped out onto the sidewalk to start her own acting career.

X X X

Mary walked a few paces down the street so that she didn't appear to be with anyone. She needed to look like a local, the neighborhood hottie, the girl that everyone had their eye on. Vin had even given her a couple of cigarettes earlier that day just in case she *really* wanted to sell that image.

Mary hadn't smoked in years; but, standing there looking aimlessly out at the quiet streets, she felt like it'd serve her appearance well. So, she reached into her small, metallic-gray backpack and pulled one out from the side zipper compartment.

Shit. I don't have a lighter! What smoker doesn't have a lighter on hand?

Her chest tightened as she looked to her left, right, and then back to her left again.

There he was, standing right outside the poker joint. Just about thirty steps from her.

Surely, if he'd just come from a room full of poker players, he'd have a lighter.

Taking a deep breath, Mary held the cigarette in between her first and middle finger and jogged towards Phil, waving her right arm gently in the air.

"Sir, sir!" she called. "Hey, do you have a—"

"NO! I don't have anything for you!" Phil snapped.

Mary stopped, catching up to herself as if her feet had arrived before her. She smiled at him, wanting to appear like she was forgiving him for already being a dick to her, or, perhaps acting as if she hadn't even heard him.

"Oh, sorry. I was just going to ask if you maybe have a lighter I could borrow really quick?"

Phil's first gander at her was judgmental, probably because she appeared to be just another street rat from a distance. But now that he was really looking at her in a close distance, she saw his pupil widen.

Mary suppressed a shudder.

"Sorry, sir, to bother you," she said. "I just … I think I lost mine. And it's been a bad day … I just want to shake it off with a cigarette."

"Oh," was all Phil said.

"Yeah. I figured, if you're hanging out down there—" Mary nodded towards the small, hidden entrance to the illegal poker parlor below. "— you might smoke cigars."

Phil didn't move, just staring at her. For a second, she thought maybe he was drunk; then she remembered that he had a *thing* for young girls. She might have been twenty-seven years old, but he was — what, fifty-something? — and she had his attention in an instant. More than just his eyes were interested in her, too. She could feel that creepy-ass vibe immediately.

You got this. You got this. You fucking got this, Mary chanted in her head over and over.

"Uh, yeah. Of course, yeah." Phil shuffled through his pocket and pulled out a torch lighter, lifting it up as Mary pushed the Marlboro into her lips.

Just as he lit the cigarette for her, she coughed, ever so slightly. Mary worried for a second that it would give away the act she was putting on. Then again, she'd already told him it was a bad day, implying she wasn't a habitual smoker.

"Been a rough one, huh?" Phil asked her as he nervously ran his fingers across his receding hairline, like that was going to cover it up or make his appearance any better.

"Yeah," Mary said. "I guess that's just how Mondays go, right?"

"What's the problem?"

"I had a big interview at an advertising agency today, but it didn't go great because, well ..." She hesitated. "It just didn't." She took a drag and exhaled the smoke through one side of her mouth.

"I bet you did better than you think, kiddo." He'd called her such a name to imply he acknowledged his senior to her, although the pang of lust he felt in saying the word was superbly disturbing.

"Yeah, maybe. I guess we'll see. Thanks for the light, and the vote of confidence." She turned, wanting to look as if she had no shits to give about him. "I'm headed to grab a drink at Mitch's Bar, so I'll leave you in peace."

Mary started walking away, and she reckoned she nailed it with the way she flexed her long, toned legs and swayed her hips slightly to emphasize her perky butt. She fixed her eyes on the yellowish Impala parked about seventy-five feet away, making sure that Brad was still close.

282

"Wait!"

Phil took a few short strides to reach her, just as she turned back to him.

"What's up?" Mary asked casually.

"Can I — well, would it be okay if I joined you for a drink?"

Mary took a sweet puff of victory from that cigarette, let out a final exhale, and flicked it onto the litter-covered street.

"Of course."

Phil whipped out his phone and canceled his Uber Black ride, which Mary saw was just a minute away. She shot him a smile, and they made their way to the bar.

Chapter Forty-Four
The Final Walk
April 11, 2022

They sat down on the ripped leather barstools at Mitch's, and Phil told the bartender that his "friend" could have whatever she wanted. Mary's tight, black-banded dress had hiked up just enough to show her smooth thighs, and she noticed Phil peeking down at them often.

Ugh. Clearly, he wanted nothing more than to get in between them. It grossed her out that she had to entertain the thoughts of this literal pedophile, but she knew that, in the end, she'd be rewarded for stepping into this uncomfortable situation.

"So, what's your name?" Phil asked her as they waited for their drinks.

"Molly," Mary lied smoothly. "You?"

"I'm Phillip."

She found it a bit odd that he gave his full first name. Maybe he was acting, too trying to be a bit of himself and a bit of someone else at the same time?

I wonder if Brad's outside. Did he see me go in — has he moved the car any closer? Just in case this doesn't work out how we planned ...

X X X

Mary and Phil chatted over their drinks for a good fifteen minutes.

"How about a shot?" she suggested.

Phil agreed, apparently without so much as a thought, and ordered another round to follow the shots. Once they'd downed them, he excused himself to go to the bathroom.

Here goes nothing.

Mary leapt into action, leaning over the bar in such a way that her cleavage was exposed to the guy behind it. She folded her arms and squeezed them against her body, pushing her tits together.

"Hey, you, can we get another round?" she asked with a wink.

As the server — now wide-eyed — poured the drinks, Mary looked behind her several times to make sure Phil hadn't come back. The clock was ticking, and the last thing she needed was this asshole pulling beers to take his time.

The bartender set the glasses down. Mary took a quick, final glance toward the bathroom. Still no Phil.

Mary fished in the zip pouch of her backpack, forcing her features into a confused expression. Her fingers closed around the small vial of Succinylcholine that Brad had given her earlier. Her heart thumped.

The server stepped away to take another patron's order; and, with a shrug, she dumped the liquid into the glass to the right of her own. Stashed the container back into her bag.

Phil returned just seconds later.

"I ordered us another round," Mary said cheerily, taking a sip of her beer and praying it would hide her nerves. "Hope that's okay."

Phil sat back down on the stool, put his hand on her knee, and said, "Of course."

It took a couple of minutes for Mary's heart to stop beating so damn hard — and it wasn't helped at all by the sick feeling in her stomach brought on by this creep *touching* her. Luckily, Phil didn't seem to notice any of her obvious anxiety. Maybe he was already a little drunk.

Mary kept up with the lighthearted banter, but she knew she'd eventually have to show a level of interest in him so he wouldn't question her intentions. Why else would this gorgeous girl be out with this old man, anyway, unless it was the result of some illegal, or super-nefarious, shit?

Phil's hand had crept up a bit, from her knee to her mid-thigh, and Mary decided it was time to reciprocate a bit. Swallowing down her disgust, she placed her hand on top of his, and, ever so slightly, moved it just about an inch toward her pussy.

The drugs hadn't quite kicked in — Phil was still decently alert. She needed that sweet spot, where he'd seem drunk but still able to stand; and he *had* to look like he'd left with her willingly.

I cannot wait to dump this asshole.

"Whaaaa, sorry … What's your hometin?" Phil slurred his next question, which was just on the edge of intelligibility.

"Sea—ashore," Mary replied, wincing internally at the drawn-out "a". "Just a small town in Florida. Sure you've never heard of it."

"Nahhh. I like Miami."

Time to go, while he while he could still form a coherent answer.

"Want to get out of here?" she asked him, with a suggestive tone.

Phil swayed a little in his seat, and she slid her hand up the leg of his dress pants, just barely close enough to his balls to make him perk up as much as he could in his altered state.

Shit. What if I have to carry him out of here?

There were only about five other people in the bar, and the likelihood of *her* being considered the villain in this situation would be astronomically low, but still ...

"A'ight," Phil said. He handed over his credit card and paid the tab, but he didn't seem to be in the same good spirits as he was in before.

Though it reassured her that he didn't have the energy, or capacity, to try anything with her, Mary worried that she'd have to text Brad to come help her. That could totally screw up the plan, since there were bound to be cameras watching the door of the bar. But she stayed the course, and pepped Phil up with some physical touch.

You just need to get him outside and into the car. It looks like an old taxi, no-one will suspect a thing.

Slinging her arm around Phil's shoulders, she offered him her body to lean against and led him away.

The Impala pulled up as soon as they emerged. Phil was stumbling with a giddiness in his step, now, though was barely speaking a word when Mary tried to talk to him. He nearly fell into the backseat but managed to grab her hands and playfully pull her down with him. Mary giggled, feeling safe to keep playing her role with Brad in the front.

X X X

Zwickel Station apartment complex was a fifteen-minute drive away. Brad didn't say a word as the engine kicked in and they started to move, but Mary saw him keeping a close eye on her in the rearview mirror.

Phil lay like a drunk-ass teenage girl across the stained, ripped cloth. He even slurred a few inappropriate advances at Mary, but she shrugged them off, since he was evidently too screwed up to get anywhere.

They crossed the railroad tracks slowly and crept the car up to Apartment E, parking as close as they could without being too visible. Brad stepped out first, and Mary followed soon after.

She walked around the car to meet Brad. Looked at him in awe of what they had just accomplished.

"What the…?" she said, glancing through the backseat window at Phil's nearly motionless form. "He's totally out. How do we do this now?"

"Don't worry. I've got this under control."

He opened up the driver's backseat door, where Phil's head was resting on the armrest — until Phil's entire upper body slid out, snakelike, and landed with a *smack* on the concrete.

Brad giggled, and it was all Mary could do to cover her mouth with her hand and turn her head away.

"Oh my God," she half-whispered with her own, albeit inappropriate, belly laugh.

"We gotta compose ourselves," Brad replied, barely smothering his own laughter.

"Right, right." Mary returned to Brad's side, trying to keep her face serious.

"I'll lift him up, you do your best to seduce him into a more conscious state, cool?" Brad asked.

"Yeah, I got you."

Brad ended up needing some support from Mary to grab Phil's heavy-ass frame and pull him up to a standing position. Phil started to grumble a little bit, so Mary took that opportunity to try to keep him intrigued enough to go into the studio.

Not far, now. Just another thirty steps or so.

"Alright. You doing okay, handsome?" she asked Phil, when she noticed his eyes had cracked open a tiny bit.

"Let's get into my place and have some fun."

"Ggggnnn—ahhh," was his only reply, in a gurgle.

At least he was standing on his own two feet. Mary wasn't too sure if she could wrangle him into the studio by herself; but she had to try. Brad couldn't be too involved, after all.

She put her arms around Phil, squeezing into him the motivation to walk the paces that would be his *final walk.*

Chapter Forty-Five
Midnight
April 11, 2022

Brad slammed on the brake, and the car skidded into the driveway. The entire ride back from the apartment, they'd had a back-and-forth commentary characterized by a combination of triumph and shock.

Mary had never done anything like that before in her entire life. She felt empowered, she said; for once, she felt like she contributed to a bigger purpose. She admitted that she loved that feeling of doing wrong when she knew it was right.

"We gotta get some sleep," Brad said as he killed the engine. "I mean, we probably have a lot of driving to do after tomorrow."

"Ugh, I know."

It sounded daunting, especially since they'd just made the long drive up, in disguise, with fake passports and all. Brad knew that the last week's activities were all completely outside of Mary's comfort zone, but she'd taken to them as if it was in her nature. He was proud of her — and it made him love her even more. To appear innocuous, while also acting with intentional conviction, was a rare trait that not many people possessed.

Even though their relationship was a complete setup from the start, Brad didn't even think of it like that anymore, and neither did Mary. He'd already told her all about how Vin had arranged for them to meet at the bar — and he'd even confessed that he was nervous that night, not because of his mission, but because he wasn't entirely sure if a girl like her would even go for a guy like him.

"My stomach was fluttering the moment Vin showed me a photo of you," he'd said to her. "I chalked it up to nerves, but ..."

But, Brad knew deep down that it hadn't been so simple. The way he'd felt was all to do with her as a person. Right from the start, it was something real: he just hadn't known it, then, because he hadn't experienced it.

Now, though, he had.

Mary looked at the clock on her phone. "It's midnight."

"Shit. Today's the day." Brad felt nineteen years of pent-up anger mustering inside him.

"I know, hun. I'm just... really sad, and sorry about everything."

"We're doing the right thing."

"It feels super wrong. This isn't anything I ever imagined I would do. But, for once, I actually feel like I matter," Mary admitted.

"You do matter, Mare," Brad assured her. "Especially to me. Soon, we're going to be living our dream. You and me. We'll have everything, and we will *be* everything." He leaned his cheek softly against hers.

"A dream wedding, a romantic and insanely preposterous honeymoon, a company that is *ours* ... We're going to make it so big and help so many people. Just think about what we'll be able to do with all that money."

Mary pressed closer to Brad as she dreamt about everything she'd never had but had always wanted.

"I always thought I'd have to climb the ladder to make a success out of myself," she said quietly. "But I think … being part of this, with you guys, it's good for me. You're like a second family. Just a bit scrappier than my folks up north."

Brad slid an arm around her, and they sat in the car for a while, the only sound that of their breathing.

Chapter Forty-Six
Chains
April 12, 2022

Phil's eyes slowly peeled open, nearly tearing lashes out from being so crusted-over. His face felt like worms were crawling across every pore, and his limbs were tingling all over.

There was no mirror in front of him; but, as Phil tried to stand, he felt as if he were watching his own movements in some freakish out-of-body experience. He was determined to focus on his surroundings, yet everything looked distorted, pixelated.

He quickly realized that standing up was not an option.

From what he could tell, there weren't many objects in the room. A bright orange smudge stood in front of him, to his left; a long piece of what he assumed was wood to his right.

Phil's brain felt like it wanted to bust out through his skull. He squinted, hoping to make even some sense of what he was seeing. Was that an old construction sawhorse with a cheap panel board sitting on top of it? Was there something on the wood — blood? No, a *face?*

It appeared to be a red canvas, upon which was painted, in dark tones, a grisly, deformed face with a contraption of some sort over the head. Maybe a reverse bear trap, or a vice.

Trapped, huh. Exactly how I feel.

Maybe this wasn't even real. Maybe he was so out of it that he was hallucinating. Was this all a dream?

Phil tried one last time to rise, but he didn't even make it onto his knees. His left hip hit the carpet first, and the rest of him soon followed as he rolled onto his back.

As his neck gave in to the lethargy, and as his head dropped and his vision started to slur, he noticed a plate of food next to him. A small bologna-and-cheese sandwich and a yogurt, with a plastic spoon, resting on a plate.

Without a thought, Phil picked up the yogurt and started to eat. He was starving, he realized — perhaps getting a little something inside him would give him at least enough energy and strength to get out of this shithole.

The bologna sandwich grossed him out a bit. He managed a few bites of the pitiful thing, and left about half of it on the plate. He still felt woozy.

Where the fuck am I? What just happened?

His mind began to race, shuffling through millisecond-like clips of what he'd done the night before. He remembered being at the poker parlor and winning a few thousand bucks. He remembered walking outside and meeting a pretty young girl whose brains he definitely wanted to bang the shit out of.

He remembered taking her to that bar down the street — the one he'd never been to before and had sworn he'd never go in, since it had such a ghetto vibe.

Why did I go there? He shut his eyes tight and thought. *Did I bang that girl? Is that where I am right now? What was her name again? Molly?*

With his head clearing up a bit, and his body just starting to catch up with his head, Phil's arms and legs started to regain feeling. His ankle started to feel heavy, as if something was bearing weight on it.

"OH MY GOD!" he screamed.

His ankles were bound together by cast-iron rings, connected together, and the accompanying chains were tied to a pipe. He wanted to use every bit of air in his lungs to blast out an audible cry for help, but suddenly found his voice powerless, as if it was dying.

What the hell is happening ...?

X X X

The next few days were all a blur. Phil would come to realize he had been abducted, try to starve himself because he realized his food was poisoned, then suffer from such heightened anxiety that he would have to drink from the bottled water that had been set out beside him. But even that had been tainted with Succinylcholine, and he'd soon succumb to paralysis once more.

It was a vicious cycle — and it was a mercy each time he, inevitably, passed out.

Chapter Forty-Seven
Day Date
April 12, 2022

Myer woke up in his lavish California king bed, looked over and saw Allie's naked body tangled up in the silky, soft sheets. They had gone out the night before for some drinks at a swanky cocktail bar, and he'd been waiting for months to get her into bed.

"Morning," he rasped.

Allie groaned and rolled over, evidently not quite awake yet.

"I need coffee," she murmured.

Myer stretched over her and leaned down to pick up his phone. A few clicks later, and Francine was making a pot of coffee for the two of them in the kitchen a few rooms over.

"Last night was fun, huh?"

Allie grinned. "Oh, yeah. I needed that so much."

They rolled around the bed for a few minutes before finally emerging and covering up in robes. Walking through the large French doors into the hallway that led to the dining room, Allie smelled the aroma of freshly ground coffee beans in the air.

Myer, who was following close behind her, took a seat at the table — the one where, just two days ago, detectives were questioning him about his assistant's disappearance in Mexico.

"Creamer or sugar?" Francine asked Allie.

"Creamer, please. Thank you," Allie said as she sat down opposite Myer.

Francine soon served up their delicious brews, and Myer asked Allie what she had on her agenda for the day, given that it was, technically, a workday.

304

"I think I'm gonna play hooky today. I need a day off, been working way too much lately."

"Sounds good." Myer smiled, but it didn't quite reach his eyes.

"What's up?"

"I'm still worried about Mary. She's been missing for three days now." Myer's face scrunched up a bit.

"Maybe she just needed to take a break from the city life," Allie suggested. "Go explore some nature. No phone, no people. LA life can be overwhelming, you know."

"True. But I can't believe she wouldn't let someone know."

"Millennials." Allie sipped her coffee and lifted her shoulders, as if to imply she felt the generation was a bit entitled.

"How about we head out for lunch?" she said, returning the cup to its coaster. "I've heard the Corsair Engine

Works is pretty cool. They used to make autos there back in the 1900s."

"Huh. I didn't know that."

"It still has a bunch of the original equipment, and it's a hotspot for local entrepreneurs. Shops, restaurants, bars, you name it." Allie pushed her cup aside, leaned across the table with her chin propped on her hands. "Whaddya say?"

"Sure." Myer wasn't overly eager; but he had to admit he was intrigued. He did have more than a passing interest in cars.

"It's about thirty minutes from here," Allie said. "Want to go around eleven?"

"Alright. Just meet me here and we'll take the car."

What he meant was that he'd have his driver take them in his private black car.

Allie agreed, standing up to head back to the bedroom to redress. Just as she left, she gave him a kiss.

"Be back in a couple hours."

X X X

Allie's Uber pulled up down the driveway, at the gate, and she was on her way back to the cocktail bar to pick up her car and head home to get ready.

She didn't really want Myer's driver involved in their plans, even though he'd likely stay in the driver's seat of the car waiting the entire time. But if she hadn't gone along with that plan, it might have made Myer suspicious; so, she figured she'd just have to deal with any complications as and when they arose.

As she climbed out of the rideshare, she texted Vinsetta.

All good for the 11:00 audition.

Her phone buzzed a moment later.

See you then.

Chapter Forty-Eight
Corsair
April 12, 2022

Waking up next to Lark, on the morning of the day that she had been waiting for pretty much her entire life, was the best damn feeling in the world to Vin. The funny thing, she thought, about all of those years of insane plotting was that she'd had no idea it would lead her to find *her person*. Even though it had been just a little less than a week, they had this whirlwind, Jack-and-Rose-from-*Titanic* sort of love story.

But I'd definitely have shared my piece of driftwood. One attempt to share that space was not *enough.*

Before Vin could even say her good mornings to Lark, he burrowed his face into her chest and began to lick her nipples. Nothing turned her on more than having her tits sucked, licked or played with, so it was welcome surprise foreplay, especially with her mind being much clearer than it was the night before.

It didn't take long for Lark's perfect penis to enter her. She desperately needed to ride him hard to get in some thrilling orgasms before the big day; and, as guilt-ridden as she should have felt with so much "wrongdoing" on the horizon, Vin didn't give in to that obligatory shame.

She let herself enjoy his body, gliding her clit over the shaft of his cock until she came at least three times. Just after her finale, Vin flexed her legs and placed her feet on the bed, one on each side of Lark's hips. She watched as she slowly moved her pelvis up and down, dominating him like a joystick. Lark's eyes met hers whenever she looked up, and Vin felt a connection that was almost impossibly deep: not just from his being inside her, but between their very souls.

Soon, his attention switched to his soaking-wet cock as he released a huge load inside her. He didn't make a sound.

This isn't just sex. It's making love.

Vin laid her head on Lark's chest, still straddling him as she felt him become flaccid beneath her stomach.

"You ready for today?" he asked, his fingers sweeping through her hair.

"I'm ready. For today, for tomorrow, for every day after that."

Vin got up, took a shower, and donned her favorite tee shirt from when she was a teenager: one she'd bought at a Matchbox Twenty concert she and Lauren had gone to in the summer of 2003. It wasn't surprising that it still fit her, since it was such a loose style.

Vin had always known that she'd wear it on this day, in honor of her soul sister.

"Nice shirt," Lark teased when she came out of the bathroom.

"Very funny, Sir Author. You think I care that they're kinda outdated? I love this shirt."

Vin pulled her jeans on and tugged at the retro tee until it stretched past her fly. She was comfortable and felt on top of the damn world. Lark, meanwhile, picked up the thick three-ring binder that had been lying on the chair next to Vin's vanity since they arrived. He hugged it close to his torso, his handsome face set with determination.

"Got it. Let's go."

As they headed out, no longer in disguise, Vin felt her phone vibrate. It was a text from Brad.

OTW.

Yesss! She typed up a quick reply of "same."

It was just past ten o'clock.

X X X

The drive to Corsair flew by. They pulled up outside the brick-and-cast-iron building, parking the Genesis on the street, at 10:50 AM.

Perfect.

Vin pushed open the main door — a heavy, solid masterpiece of dark oak. Her mind flashed back to the epiphany she'd had at Lark's apartment a couple days prior, and she smiled as she recalled the lyrics to that monumental song.

This is the end.

They had the perfect amount of time to get inside and station themselves in the warehouse of the distillery. Allie's friend from high school owned the bar there, and he'd agreed to let her use the free storage space for one of her design projects. Since it —and the whole building — didn't officially open until 1:00 PM, he'd told her he'd just use that extra time to do paperwork in his office.

Of course, Allie had discreetly passed all this info on to Vin; and she'd sure as hell never have revealed that there'd be nobody else around when she convinced Myer to grab lunch with her. Nor did Vin expect that Myer would bother to look up the Corsair's opening hours.

At the entrance to the warehouse, they paused. A long, deep breath escaped from Vin's mouth.

"You okay?" Lark asked.

"I'm good, yeah. Nervous, but I'm still confident."

"I've got you," he said, slipping a hand from around his binder and taking hold of Vin's. She squeezed his fingers in turn, and they entered the room where the showdown was all set to happen.

Two windows at the far side provided the only light, which caused the loose particles of dust hovering in the air to shimmer. It was a wide-open space with a door on each side: one by the front where you could exit and enter the main bar area, and another in the back from which you'd step outside into a gravel parking lot.

Vin walked Lark across the cement floor, watching out for rusty nails or debris, and flipped up the catch on the deadbolt lock. A few tugs made it give way with a squeal.

They froze. Waited.

Nothing.

Vin wrapped her hand around the doorknob and pulled. Luckily, the metal slab swung aside with little effort.

She exchanged a last glance with Lark before shutting it and taking her place by the main door.

What a journey we've already been on together. Perhaps oddly, considering the situation, butterflies stirred in her stomach. And this time, Vin was certain it was a combination of those twinges of love mixed with the anxious knots in her gut, unraveling like tiny hairs on twine.

She waited in complete silence for what felt like ages — then, she heard some rumbling in the adjacent room.

Is it him? she thought. *Is it finally time?*

Chapter Forty-Nine
Sage
April 12, 2022

Vin made sure she stuck to the shadows, a little way from the door, so Myer wouldn't realize right away that he was in deep shit and try to escape.

He trusts Allie, Vin reminded herself. *He's got no clue she's bringing him to the worst moment of his entire life.*

The hinges creaked, and Vin inhaled a huge breath. She heard Allie's voice, telling Myer that this was the coolest room of the entire building and that they *had* to check it out. He didn't rebut, or even really reply, to her.

The door slammed closed — Vin's cue.

"What is this?" Myer asked.

Vin stepped slightly forward with her right foot: the starting point of a sure-fire pivot that would reveal her profile.

"This is where you're about to make some life-changing decisions, Myer," she announced, barely stifling a smile as she spoke the words she'd been waiting to say for nineteen years.

Myer's face shriveled up with a look of confusion. Allie was now standing behind him, in front of the door, and he turned to look at her in total disbelief.

"Why aren't you in New York?" he growled, whipping back to Vin. "You had a *job*, Vinsetta."

"Oh, I completed your fucking job. Walk with me." She said with a tone she had never delivered.

Another quick turn to Allie confirmed he didn't have a choice. Myer came slowly over to Vin, and she led him in a stroll across the warehouse floor to the back door. She gave it a few taps with her knuckles.

"Stop there," Vin demanded, retreating a little and holding her free hand out to stop Myer. "I have something for you."

The door flew open, and Lark walked in. Myer's face turned as white as a paper straw wrapper. Lark pulled the binder out from under his arm and held it up over his head.

"This? *This* is what you want?" he spat, tossing it at Myer. It landed by Myer's foot, sending up spirals of dust. "There you go, you piece of shit."

Myer bent down to pick it up — feeling, no doubt, as if he had won. But no sooner had his hands brushed the cover of the folder than the front door gave another creak.

Vin watched as Myer twisted around to look; as he slowly recomposed himself, standing up while clutching Lark's manuscript to his chest.

"Who are *you*?" he asked the brown-haired woman who had assumed Allie's former position.

Time seemed to stand still for the few seconds that it took for her to situate herself next to Vin. She looked at Vin, who held her gaze deliberately — just long enough to reveal to Myer that they knew each other very well indeed.

"Why didn't you ever say anything, to anyone, about what you saw him to do me?" Sage said, her eyes snapping to Myer.

"Huh? Who?"

"You watched my dad sexually abuse me; I saw you through the window. For days, I waited and waited, thinking surely you would turn him into the police..." she shook her head at him.

"BUT YOU NEVER FUCKING DID!" Her calm demeanor quickly shifted to a scream.

Myer's hands began to shake, and he almost dropped the binder.

"Lauren?" he gasped out. "Lauren Eddy?"

Sage took four slow and dramatic steps toward him, then leaned her head to the side in the most casual, innocent way imaginable.

"Call me Sage."

Chapter Fifty
The End
April 12, 2022

Sage stood only two feet from Myer's face: the face she — and Vin — had been waiting to be spitting distance from ever since Sage had abandoned her old life and hidden herself in that shitty studio apartment.

"You saw what my father did to me," Sage went on. "I saw you. You saw me — the fear in me, we both know you did. But you didn't say *anything*."

Her voice started to crack, and Vin took over.

"You thought blackmailing me to steal Lark's manuscript was going to turn out in your favor? Let me tell you how the tables have turned, my friend.

"You only *thought* you saw me murder this incredible girl. She was, and still is, my best friend. We knew you wouldn't turn me in for what I supposedly did to her because you had too much on the line. Too much to lose."

Myer looked like his jaw would hit the concrete any second, and Vin almost laughed. Almost. She came to stand beside Sage, wrapping her arm around Sage's shoulders.

"We were fourteen," Vin continued, "and this all started out as a reason for Lauren to get out of her house and away from her abusive dad. She needed to be gone, missing, or worse — murdered, apparently. We knew you were going to be there that night, dropping off paperwork, and we were ready to destroy you. You *knew* what he did to her—" Vin's voice dropped to a snarl "— and you never said a word, not one goddamn thing.

"Obviously, you liked to watch. So we knew that you wouldn't be able to resist spectating what you thought was some teenage drama turned to slaughter. And we knew you'd never breathe a word about it. You didn't want to jeopardize the deal you had with her dad, you selfish bitch."

Sage's eyes were already watering. A few rogue tears slipped down her face, and Vin tightened her hold on Sage. Vin took a moment to glance around, saw that Lark and Allie were still standing at either end of the room, in front of the doors they'd entered by.

"You went on to be a famous, wealthy, successful Hollywood prick. You slept like a damn champion every night, even with all of this shit on your conscience. How do you think *she* slept, wondering if — *when* — her dad was going to sneak in again and violate her? Huh?"

"I …" Myer stammered. "Uh—"

"And how do you think she coped, locked inside a tiny, ghetto-ass apartment for four years - FOUR, with no communication with the outside world? All that time, before she could finally rejoin society as an adult, as a completely different person, the only people she had were me, and well …"

The door once again swung open, and in walked in Brad and Mary.

"… Brad," Vin concluded.

Brad awkwardly waved at Myer, whose mouth hung open as his gaze flicked to Mary.

"What the hell?" Myer exclaimed. "Mary? Oh my God."

"Hi, Myer," Mary said.

"You're ... Oh my God, you're here. Are you okay? What, wait... what the hell is going on?"

Mary just smiled, taking a few steps towards Myer.

"I'm missing, yeah. So is my boyfriend, Vinsetta's stepbrother." She gave Brad a look of adoration. "But guess who's guilty of kidnapping us?"

Myer had no reaction, as he appeared he was suffering from a major case of information overload.

Mary told Myer all about how she'd planted evidence in his office that he'd abducted them — and that he'd, supposedly, found out she was planning to resign and wanted to punish her for it, as well as cash-in her life insurance policy.

"That's not all you're guilty of, either," Vin chimed in.

"You see, officially, no trace of Lauren past the age of fourteen exists. I guess you could say she really did die, then. But the bloody blanket we wrapped her in? Strands of her hair, and that locket she always wore? They *do* exist. And guess where all of that is right now? In your office. All we have to do is call Detective Pearson, and you're screwed, Myer."

Slowly, Vin pulled her cell phone from her pocket; tapped the screen to bring up her contacts list and turned it to face Myer.

"Look, I have his number right here. When my stepbrother went missing in Cabo, I got calls from detectives, too."

Brad butted in with a few words of his own.

"You fucked up a lot of people's lives. I was there when we staged Lauren's murder. All three of us — me, Vin, and Sage — were in this together. We're the team you don't mess with. Got it?"

"What do you want?" Myer asked, finally finding his voice, his eyes darting between the five of them.

Vin, Sage, Lark, Brad, and Mary all quickly exchanged looks.

This is it.

"I'll start." Brad gave a quick nod. "That reward of five million dollars we'd get if we turned you in for Lauren's murder? Yeah, we want that. Otherwise, we never turn up, and you get pegged for our disappearance."

"You want five million dollars? You have to be joking."

"Yeah, and that's not all." Vin jumped in. "You've got what you wanted, what you thought was your big prize — Lark's manuscript. I want the lead in the movie. If you don't agree to give me that, I'll turn you in for murdering Lauren."

Mary stood there shaking her head. "We're ready to drive that piece-of-shit car back to Cabo and turn up totally alive," she said. "Or, we pull our own "Lauren": change our identities and never return. You sure you want to go to prison for three murders on top of abduction?"

Silence fell and stayed for what felt like an uncomfortably long time.

Lark stepped up.

"You're better off taking care of this shit, man," he said.

"What's five million bucks to you, anyway? My new book is gold, you already know that, or you wouldn't have tried to steal it. You're already a rich prick and once you turn it into a movie, you'll be even richer."

Myer's features took on an expression of defeat.

"Fine. Vinsetta, I'll give you the damn lead and Larkland, you can even be the director. Mary, Brad, I'll give you the damn money."

Myer threw his hands up, paused and looked around, as did Vin. Her face, along with the rest of the groups', was a mask of seriousness.

"I get it," Myer said after a few awkward moments. "Nice work."

Another silence.

"So …" Myer began in a different tone. "If Phil is the one who caused all this chaos, what's his punishment?"

Lark and Allie appeared confused, discontented, and everyone else followed suit.

Those two, and Myer — they have no idea, Vin thought.

Really, neither she, nor Sage, Brad, or Mary, had prepared to answer a question like that. Perhaps that was the only flaw in their otherwise-airtight plan.

Even though Vin's acting skills were always on point, and improvising should have been something she was skilled at, she found herself without anything to say. Thankfully, Sage spoke up.

"Karma."

They shot looks of agreement at one another, leaving Myer standing dumbstruck.

"It's awfully hot in hell," Sage added with a shrug.

Chapter Fifty-One
Cheers
April 12, 2022

Brad and Mary hopped in their Impala and started the twenty-four-hour drive back to Cabo. Meanwhile, Myer rode off in his black car to, like a first grader, go think about everything he'd done wrong — at least, that was what Vin liked to think happened.

That left only Vin, Lark, and Sage; and Allie, who, while not necessarily on bad terms with Myer, didn't want to be anywhere near him while he processed the massive blackmail they'd all just delivered to him. So, she stayed behind at Corsair with the others.

"What now?" Lark was the first to voice what, no doubt, most of them were thinking.

Vin smiled, sidling up to Allie.

"How about we ask that buddy of yours if we can snag a beer before he opens? We do have a hell of a lot to celebrate."

x x x

A few minutes later, they were raising their freshly filled mugs in a toast. Vin looked directly at Sage and said, "This. This is for you."

The tears finally flooded from Sage's eyes as she burst out sobbing. Everyone else took a sip of their beer, but Sage went over to Vin and buried her head in Vin's shoulder. Vin wrapped her arms tightly around Sage.

"I told you," she said, her own voice breaking a little, "I will *always* take care of you."

Sage wept and wept, and Vin comforted her. A few feet away, she overhead Lark and Allie making small talk. Allie was telling him how she'd come to be Vin's agent, about her experiences over the years — and, of course, how much she admired the work of her favorite author.

Sage eventually composed herself together enough to celebrate with the drink she'd deserted on the table.

"Thank you, thank you all," she called out, lifting up her beer, "more than you will ever know."

They all clanked the glasses together and drank. Lark looked across the small, round table at Vin with, she thought, newfound appreciation, like everything he'd just witnessed had proved to him that her loyalty to those whom she loved was no joke. She could feel him falling even harder for her, as if he knew that being her partner in life would mean he'd always have someone he could trust at his back.

Chapter Fifty-Two
Lauren
May 15, 2022

A month later, Vin was back in New York with Lark. They'd decided to spend some time together there while Myer was working to get the movie's pre-production underway.

Just as she was about to head out to the airport to fly back to LA, Lark grabbed her waist and pulled her close.

"I love you," he said earnestly. "Everything about you. The way you care for the people in your life that matter the most to you, the way you love me — and I know you do."

Vin hadn't told him that she loved him yet, but the fact that he already knew was seriously adorable.

"I do," was all she said as she gazed up at him, kissed him, and walked out the door.

X X X

As soon as her flight landed, Vin texted Brad.

Hey bro. You and Mary free to grab dinner later? Can't wait to catch up and hear about the new company.

One of the reasons Brad had wanted that big reward was because it'd give him the means to start his own talent agency for musicians; and he'd just started getting it all set up. He'd hired Sage to handle his marketing and design, offering to pay her two million dollars for her services.

Yep, Brad replied. Needs to be later, though, how about 9?

That's a plan. See you then. Inviting Sage, too.

Sweet. The band back together. Love it!

It felt weird to be back at her house all by herself. She'd always loved that life, before, being single and doing whatever she wanted. To think that she'd now found a companion, someone she really wanted to be by her side all the time ... It was taking some getting used to.

Vin lounged around the house for a few hours, watching some raunchy, shameless TV, waiting for the stroke of eight so she could start preparing. The time seemed to pass as slow as a snail on a mud run course; but, at long last, her alarm went off, and she shook off the long day to go get dressed.

X X X

Vin drove out to meet up with the old crew, super excited to see Sage, who she hadn't gotten together with since that day at Corsair.

As she sat at the table, waiting for the others to arrive, she was startled by a series of sudden footsteps followed by a slight tickle on her arms.

"Ahh, girl! So happy to see you!"

Vin spun around to seize her in a hug. Her friend was dressed in nearly the exact same outfit: yoga pants, a tank top, sneakers and a headband. It looked a tad out of place even in this casual joint; but it was the most appropriate attire they had, considering they had a bit of exercise ahead of them.

"Just waiting on Brad and Mary, now," Vin added.

They settled in with a couple drinks, chatting it up and laughing, until Vin spotted a familiar mop of blond hair by the door and jumped up. He approached with Mary, with whom he still made the cutest damn couple ever — and there were smiles and embraces all round.

The four of them gabbed for over an hour at this tiny little joint not far from Zwickel Station. It was just on the outskirts of the rigid area, so they didn't necessarily fit in, nor did they really stand out. The guy who owned this divey restaurant was a friend of Warwick's.

"You guys ready?" Vin asked at last.

They all nodded.

"Let's go," Sage growled with her lips pursed.

X X X

Snapping her pair of plastic gloves back over her hands, Sage grabbed the large red canister with a long black nozzle from her car and transported it over to Vin's Genesis as Brad and Mary climbed into the backseat.

On the quick drive over to Zwickel, Mary said, "I don't know how he's faring. All I've done is push a plate of shitty food and a bottle of water inside the door every day for the last month."

"Yeah, and all the news about his disappearance is totally pointing the finger at his soon-to-be ex-wife," Brad added. "Especially since she had just found out about his child porn obsession — Shit. Sorry, Sage."

"It's okay, Brad," Sage replied. "You know what I think of him, and my mom. She knew what he did to me all those years. I feel nothing."

"The fact that she took out a big life insurance policy on him just adds motive. Even though she's saying it was because she found out he was sick," Brad said.

"True." Vin glanced at her rearview mirror, giving them a look of affirmation, as they rolled up to the eerily empty apartment complex. Warwick had completed his task of moving all the tenants out, so no-one was coming around there much anymore.

Sage stepped out first, her eagerness almost overwhelming and terrifying. She'd always been the super-sweet girl who wouldn't hurt even a fly; but right now, she wanted revenge. Vin could see it in every sinew of Sage's body, feel it in her damn soul.

This isn't Sage, Vin thought. *It's Lauren.*

Brad, Mary and Vin followed closely behind Sage as she took every vengeful step towards the building, watched as she poured gasoline around the entire perimeter. They'd come thinking that they would have to aid in this mission, but Sage was clearly determined to do this herself.

When the can was emptied, Sage stormed up to the door of her former jail cell, leaned her whole body against it, and screamed at the top of her lungs.

Just as she ran out of air and her voice became quiet, there came a cry from inside.

"Please, please… Hello? Please, someone. Let me go…"

Sage took a step back, threw the can as hard as she could to her right, and thrust her hands against the bright-blue door, pounding on it while she screeched:

"You never let me go! YOU NEVER LET ME GO! I *begged* you to let me go and you *never* FUCKING let me go!"

Vin couldn't help bawling. Sage, Lauren — whoever she was now and might be after — was her best friend. To see this moment, where over twenty-eight years of pain and anguish was released, was monumental and tormenting. Vin's heart broke for her.

They would never know if Phil recognized the voice of his own daughter, standing outside that door; and Vin doubted that any of them cared. She certainly didn't.

Sage stepped away from the door, put her hand deep inside her waistline pocket, and pulled out a book of matches.

"Stand back," she ordered the others, like this shit was her own daytime talk show.

"Wait, Sage!" Vin called out. "Sage, sweetie? Are you sure you're—"

"I'm Lauren."

Sage ripped a match from the small book, swiped it across the pad, and tossed it onto the floor where she'd drenched the gasoline.

The four of them stood there and watched for a couple of minutes as the complex started to go up in flames.

X X X

Two days later, Vin flew back to New York to be with Lark.

"Karma," was all she told him of her meeting with their fellow accomplices, just as the news of Phil Eddy's sex-worker-kidnapping-turned-murder broke across every single media outlet.

338

Chapter Fifty-Three
The Award
January 2024

"You look more stunning than ever, Vin," Lark said to her as they were just about to leave for the evening. They'd already had a glass of champagne together, and the night was super young.

The limo drove the newly married couple to The Beverly Hills Hotel, and they damn near made out the entire drive.

"I'm super proud of you," he whispered, pressing his forehead against hers. He'd become the one person she wanted to hear that from the most, since he'd become so much more than just her partner in crime.

"Well, this is your story, and you are my soulmate," Vin whispered back. "So it felt pretty natural to play out your script."

The pair stepped out of the limo onto the red carpet, together, as director and actress. Swathes of fans gathered around, trying to get their attention and screaming in awe.

For the first time, Larkland Rozsak was truly recognizable in public.

They kept their strut as modest as possible, stopping occasionally for photos and interviews with TV hosts, magazine reps, and journalists.

X X X

A couple hours later, Vin sat anxiously beside Lark in the audience hall, as Jennifer Aniston took to the podium to announce the Best Leading Actress award.

Vin's palms were sweating, and she grew more agitated with each nominee that was read out. All of these actresses were downright amazing — veteran professionals — and hearing her own name included on that list was surreal.

"And the award goes to ..." Aniston opened the glittering envelope, drew out the card which bore the name of the winner. "Vinsetta Davis!"

Vin's heart dropped. She looked at Lark, thunderstruck, and saw him mouth, "I love you."

Holy shit.

Slowly, Vin got to her feet. Brad and Mary, who were sitting behind her, stood up and applauded; and Brad reached over to give her a high-five. Sage and Barry both lifted their champagne glasses to toast her as she almost wobbled towards the aisle.

Just after she brushed past Lark, Allie looked up at her and said, "Proud of you, girl."

Vin didn't have a ton of time to reply, since she needed to get her ass up on that stage; but she met Allie's eyes with a smile and replied, "Thank you."

X X X

Allie felt she could take credit for Vinsetta's success, since she'd been her agent for over twenty years.

And as she ran her fingers over the diamond tennis bracelet that Kathy had gifted her before her death, she leaned over and whispered into Myer's ear:

"We did it."

Made in the USA
Monee, IL
12 December 2022

21038112R00204